LONE TRAIL'S END

Five years earlier, Grace Hammond wouldn't marry Pete Marsh, a mere cowhand. But now Pete, a prosperous rancher, has returned. However, a range war rages between Hammond, Grace's father, and his rival, Dyson. Hammond wants Dyson jailed and Pete agrees to join the fight. Then Dyson's top gun is sent out to finish Pete, who has been sworn in as deputy. He is the law and must bring the killers to justice, and face his own destiny . . .

DAVID GUEST

◆

LONE TRAIL'S END

Complete and Unabridged

LINFORD
Leicester

First published in Great Britain in 2000

First Linford Edition
published 2010

Originally published in paperback as
Gunsmoke Valley by James Marshal

The moral right of the author has been asserted

British Library CIP Data

Guest, David, *1920* –
 Lone Trail's end. - -
 (Linford western library)
 1. Western stories.
 2. Large type books.
 I. Title II. Series III. Marshal, James.
 Gunsmoke Valley.
 823.9'14–dc22

ISBN 978–1–44480–321–1

Published by
F. A. Thorpe (Publishing)
Anstey, Leicestershire

Set by Words & Graphics Ltd.
Anstey, Leicestershire
Printed and bound in Great Britain by
T. J. International Ltd., Padstow, Cornwall

This book is printed on acid-free paper

1

Violence

The shack had a sinister air. It squatted back from the trail, shadowed by gaunt, leafless pines, timbers sagging and the only window boarded up. A cold wind whistled eerily between the trees and the sullen sky, heavy with snow clouds, pressed down like a dark shroud.

Pete Marsh saw the shack and reined in his horse. He sat motionless in the saddle, watching the place from the shadows. There was no light showing, no sound from within, no movement except the creak of branches in the wind. The shack looked forlorn and forgotten.

Marsh studied the warped, unpainted timbers with a calculating eye. Someone has lived there, someone who was not there now. It promised shelter for

1

the night, food, a fire, a bed away from the bitterness of an Arizona winter. Yet he had a feeling of uneasiness. His right hand closed over the butt of his revolver as he called:

'Anyone at home?'

No voice answered him. Only the sighing wind disturbed the silence. He called a second time, and remained unanswered. His horse shifted restively, disturbing dry cones with its hoofs. He rubbed the side of the horse's muzzle, and murmured:

'Steady, Starlight — steady, boy!'

The sable gelding with the white marking stopped pawing the ground. Marsh slid out of the saddle, left Starlight's reins trailing the long grass, and moved towards the shack. He made a bulky silhouette in the moonlight, a tall, well-built man with a powerful body and square shoulders. He moved purposefully across the open space in front of the hut, Stetson tipped back and showing short, dark hair, a Colt .45 in his hand.

He wore a blue shirt and chaparejos over his denim pants, a neckerchief loose at his throat. His high-heeled riding-boots were covered with a film of dust. He reached the door of the wooden shack and pushed it open, covering the dark interior with his gun. He waited, listening, then satisfied that no ambusher lay in hiding, strode inside. He found a lamp and lit it; yellow flame and oily smoke swirled up from the wick, the light striking Marsh's face. It was a hard face, with keen grey eyes and tight lines about the mouth; the angle of his jaw was strong, one cheek marked by a knife scar.

Marsh stared round the room. It was barely furnished, two thin blankets on the bunk, cold ashes in the stove, tinned food piled in one corner. There was an empty whisky bottle under the table and dust on the floor. He went outside and round the back; a lean-to with a hitching rail formed a crude stable, and there was a half-sack of oats under the water barrel.

Marsh made up his mind; he had travelled far that day and his mount was tired. He would stay the night here and go on to River Bend and the Hammond ranch in the morning. He holstered his gun and whistled softly. Starlight came trotting to find him.

He stripped off his saddle and blanket roll, rubbed down the horse and spread out a quantity of oats. The wind was rising, chill and sharp like a knife edge. Marsh re-entered the hut, adjusted the oil-lamp, and started to build a fire in the stove. He opened a tin of fat pork and beans and fried them with thick slices of bread. He made dense black coffee and rolled himself a cigarette.

He tilted back his chair, blew smoke upwards, and stared at the ceiling. He had a satisfied, comfortable feeling. It would be nice to sleep on a bunk again, after nights on the prairie. He piled more wood into the stove and listened to the crackle of the flames.

No more running, he thought, no

more ducking a sheriff's posse and riding the lone trail, sleeping under the stars with a loaded gun in his hand. Decent folk knew him in Gunsmoke Valley, people who would remember him from five years back. No one here knew he was an outlaw with a price on his head, wanted by the law in three states.

He finished his cigarette and threw the butt into the stove, frowning. He had heard rumours on the trail, rumours that made him uneasy for the Hammonds — the days of rustling and gunplay had returned. But tomorrow would be soon enough for that . . .

Marsh rose to his feet and went outside. It was dark now, with an icy wind cutting between the pines; the snow, which had been threatening all day, still held off. The winter was going to be long and hard. He walked round the shade to the lean-to. Starlight had bedded down for the night, muzzle between handsome forelegs. Marsh dragged some bracken across the

5

entrance to block off the bitter wind, and went back inside.

He took the blankets off the bunk and replaced them with his own, kicked off his boots and loosened his clothing ready for sleep. He stoked up the fire, turned down the wick in the lamp so that only a glimmer of light remained, and crawled on to the bunk.

He was a wealthy man now, not a penniless cowhand; he could afford to leave a good price for his board and lodging in the morning, knowing that whoever owned the shack would not grudge him shelter. Western hospitality was open-handed, and he would be expected to make himself at home.

His eyes closed, his breathing became heavy and regular. It had been a hard ride, and he was tired. The muscles of his body slackened. Pleasant thoughts ran through his head — thoughts of a girl with a pretty face and brown curls. He dropped off to sleep, thinking of Grace Hammond, the girl he loved and had come back to marry . . .

Rough hands grabbed him. Marsh woke suddenly, reaching automatically for his gun. Something hard and cold slammed down on his knuckles and sharp pain shot up his arm. He heard his gun hit the boards.

His eyes were wide open now, all sleepiness gone. The lamp had been turned up, and he saw three tough-looking men crowding round the bunk. The big man with the red hair grasped Marsh's injured hand and pulled: it felt as if his arm would leave the shoulder socket. Marsh hit the floor, his legs entangled with blankets, and sprawled there, gasping for air. A boot clumped into his chest, and a voice grated:

'Get up, hombre — you're not hurt yet!'

Marsh tried to reach his Colt where it lay on the floor, but another of the men kicked it across the room. Two of them jerked him upright, twisting his arms and holding them behind him. He stood unsteadily, facing the man with red hair.

'What are yuh doing here?' demanded the big man.

Marsh didn't feel like answering. He was hurt and angry. He set his jaw and glared back. A ham-like fist crashed into his face, and red-hair growled again:

'What yuh doing here? Speak up, or I'll sure spoil yore looks permanently!'

Marsh shook his head to get the mist out of his eyes. He spat blood and licked the frame of his mouth with his tongue. He didn't know who these men were, but they were tough and it was going to do him no good to antagonise them.

He said: 'I was riding through, saw this shack and made myself at home. Nothing wrong in that, is there?'

One of the men holding Marsh — a skinny runt with a lean, stubbled face and pin-point eyes — spoke softly.

'This boy thinks he's tough, Red. Hit him again to loosen him up.'

Marsh couldn't dodge with two men pinning his arms. Red's fist drove into his mouth with steam-hammer force. Marsh spat again.

'I'll settle with you one day, Red,' he grunted. 'One day when there's just the two of us and I have my hands free.'

Red struck him again.

'I'll do the talking, stranger. You just answer questions. Where yuh riding to?'

'Just through. This ain't private territory, is it?'

'Clever hombre!'

It was the third man who spoke. He was shorter than the other two, thick-set and fleshy, his clothes skin-tight and nearly bursting. He twisted Marsh's arm till the pain set beads of sweat standing out from his forehead. 'What yuh doing in the valley a-tall?' Red asked.

'I told yuh,' Marsh mumbled. 'I was riding through — '

Red spat in Marsh's face. He was a giant-sized man with a thick, bull neck and enormous hands. His face was ugly and freckled, and he was a natural bully.

9

'Waal, keep riding — strangers ain't wanted in Gunsmoke Valley!'

The fleshy man sniggered in Marsh's ear.

'Only yuh won't be riding, hombre, 'cause I've taken a fancy to yore hoss. So yuh can walk out the way yuh came — see?'

Marsh twisted his head to look at the speaker; he had a wart on his nose and piggy eyes.

He said: 'I used a rope on the last horse-thief I met. Seems likely I'll be treating you the same way, wart-nose!'

The fleshy man snarled savagely and bent Marsh backwards. Red hit him in the belly, driving the air out of his lungs. Marsh gasped like a fish out of water.

The skinny runt said: 'He's wearing a money-belt, high up, under his armpits. Let's see what he's carrying.'

Red ripped Marsh's shirt open and fumbled with thick fingers at the belt's fastening. He pulled it away from Marsh's chest and spread it out on the table opening the pockets. His eyes gleamed with avarice.

'Say, this hombre's well heeled . . . '

He flipped through the greenbacks, counting rapidly. He whistled shortly.

'Close on two thousand dollars!' he announced. 'I reckon it was lucky we dropped in tonight.'

'The unluckiest thing yuh ever did,' Marsh snapped. 'I'll make a point of meeting up with you hombres again.'

Red laughed unpleasantly.

'Then we must see what we can do to put that idea out of yore head. Hold him tight — '

As Red balled his fists and moved in to strike, Marsh leant back, throwing his weight on the two men holding him. His right foot shot out and caught Red, doubling him over with agony.

Wart-nose cursed and grabbed for his gun. Marsh tried to break free but the skinny runt was stronger than he looked. The barrel of a .45 came crashing down on Marsh's skull, driving the strength out of his body. His legs buckled under him and he slid to the floor.

He was not unconscious, but neither did he have the power to get up. He lay there, dazed, a red mist over his eyes and his brain thudding like an Indian tom-tom. Red had recovered; he stood over Marsh, virulent abuse streaming from his lips, kicking him till Marsh thought his ribs must cave in. He rolled over, trying ineffectively to hold Red's ankles. Again and again heavy boots smashed into his body. A blackness began to spread across his consciousness. Red's words came faintly to his ears:

'Hold him up, you guys — I haven't finished with him yet!'

Marsh was dimly aware of being hauled upright. He sagged limply, his head lolling on his chest. A hand from behind yanked at his hair, pulling his head up and exposing his face. Red came in, fists pounding like pistons, hammering agony into Marsh's face.

The other two released their hold

and Marsh hit the floor again. It was an effort to try to crawl away.

Red said: 'All right, throw him out!'

The fleshy man took Marsh's arms, the skinny runt his legs. Marsh was suspended over the floor, bowed, helpless. Red opened the door and a bitter wind whistled through. The two men carrying Marsh swung him back and forward, let him go. Marsh curved through the air and hit the ground.

Red called from the doorway.

'Start running, hombre. Get out of Gunsmoke Valley — and stay out. We don't like strangers here!'

Marsh climbed to his knees. Through a blur, he saw that Red had a gun in his hand. Flame stabbed the darkness and a slug furrowed the earth and ricochetted past him. He swayed upright, turning. Red fired again, and a third time.

'Run, fellar, run,' he shouted.

The bullets passed between Marsh's legs as he stumbled away.

The skinny runt's voice followed after him jeering: 'Here's yore boots, stranger.

Use 'em to make tracks out of the valley.'

He threw them, one after the other, at Marsh. The first caught the side of his head and knocked him flat again; the other landed yards away. Red's gun blasted lead, smashing the rowel on the boot Marsh picked up and held in his hand. Marsh ran crookedly, like a drunken man, his head reeling. He got the other boot and made for the cover of the trees. Red emptied the chambers of his gun after him, then shouted:

'Can't yuh go any faster? Get out — and get fast!'

Marsh reached the trees and took shelter. Red and the other two had gone back inside the hut. The door closed after them; the sound of raucous laughter came on the night air.

Marsh put on his boots and started walking away from the shack. A cold wind whip-lashed his body and he shivered. He had to keep moving; if he lay down he would freeze to death. Farther on, he found a creek. The water was crystal clear and icy cold, but it revived him. He bathed his face and washed off the blood, took a long drink, then sat on a tree stump resting his aching muscles.

There was a moon, and the silvery light showed brown grassland stretching flatly to the horizon. Dark clouds hung heavily. A few flakes of snow drifted down. Marsh stood up, flexing his hands: there was hot anger in him. He wanted to go right back and deal out some punishment himself, but he was in no condition for that. His head cleared, and reason came to him.

He couldn't deal with three armed thugs, alone and without a gun. He would need to wait, but he'd go back to that shack. He'd lost his horse, his money-belt, his guns. There was nothing he could do but walk for the town, and keep walking, hoping he wouldn't drop from exhaustion before he got there.

But he'd go back, he promised himself. He'd go back with a gun in his hand and Red would get what was coming to him.

The wind keened across the prairie, chilling Marsh's skin and threatening to freeze him solid if he didn't keep putting one foot in front of the other. He plodded on, looking for landmarks. He was south of the river that split the valley, at the eastern end, farthest from the Hammond ranch. He aimed for River Bend and swung his arms to keep his circulation going.

Gunsmoke Valley was a cleft in high tableland, fifty miles long and varying ten to fifteen miles wide. It had lush pastureland and could support a heavy beef herd — no scrub and sand here. There were trees, too, pine and cottonwood on the sloping hillsides, aspens bordering the creeks that fed the big river.

Marsh picked up the trail to the river and kept walking, mile on mile. He remembered the oxbow, and the small town nestling in the bed of the river. He just had to keep going till he reached River Bend . . . the snow began to fall faster.

2

Lynching Party

Joe Brett was odd-job man at the Pine Roost stables. He was up early that morning, just as dawn was flushing the sky with crimson light, cleaning out the sheds and pitchforking fresh hay to the horses. He had broken the thin covering of ice on the drinking trough and was sweeping the snow from the yard when he happened to look down the length of River Bend's Main Street.

The town was quiet. A few lights gleamed from unshuttered windows, the only indication that folk were preparing to go about the day's work. Somewhere a door banged, disturbing the silence of early morning with the abruptness of a pistol shot. And down the street came a man reeling as if drunk.

Joe Brett stared at him, wondering where he'd got the liquor that soon in the day. Then he looked closer, and saw that the man was hurt. He'd come into town from the east, on foot, and he looked fit to drop in his tracks. Joe chucked his broom away and started running.

'Hold up, fellar,' he called out. 'I'm coming.'

Pete Marsh heard the words with a sense of immense relief. There was a mist over his eyes and he hardly saw the lanky arms of the odd-job man come out to grab him as he stumbled. He was cold and tired; his legs felt like cornstalks under a gale and his head was numb with the effort of keeping himself moving. He muttered thickly, 'River Bend — I made it,' and collapsed.

Joe Brett hefted Marsh across his shoulders and carried him down the street to Doc Turner's house. He pushed open the door and went in, dropped Marsh on a couch and started shouting for the doctor. Turner came sleepily from his bed growling:

'What in hell is it now? Can't a man get any sleep in this doggoned town?'

'Quit bawling, doc,' Brett drawled. 'Yuh got a case.' He nodded towards the couch.

Doc Turner took one look at Marsh and stopped moaning. He forced Marsh's mouth open and poured brandy down his throat.

'Stoke the fire up, Joe,' he said to Brett. 'This hombre's three parts frozen.'

He started using salves on Marsh's bruised and battered flesh, wrapped him in blankets and dosed him with more brandy. Brett had the fire roaring now; the temperature in the room went up till the two men began to sweat.

'Reckon he'll live?' Brett asked.

Doc Turner nodded.

'He'll live all right. He looks to me like an hombre with the constitution of a horse.' He paused, staring thoughtfully at his patient. 'What's more, I've a feeling I've seen him before.'

Joe Brett said: 'I was thinking the same. Reminds me some of Peter Marsh who used to be around these parts, four, five years ago.'

Doc Turner screwed up his eyes and squinted along the length of his beaky nose.

'You're remembering good, Joe. It is Marsh, though he's changed some with the years. He sure looks a tough boy now. Reckon he'll have a story to tell when he wakes up.'

'And I've got a job waiting,' Joe Brett drawled. 'See yuh later, doc.'

He went back to the stables, leaving Doc Turner to tend his patient.

Pete Marsh slept twenty-four hours, then woke up stiff and hungry. He wondered where he was as he dragged himself out of bed. He was unsteady on his legs, and his face felt like it had been sandpapered. He began to remember things: the shack, Red and his two cronies, taking a beating, losing Starlight and his money-belt, the walk to River Bend. He got that far when Doc Turner came into the room.

'What d-yuh think you're doing out of bed?' the doctor asked. 'Don't you know better than to walk around in yore state of health? I'm Doc Turner in case you're aiming to pay my bill.'

'I'll pay yuh, doc, in due course, and thanks for looking after me. The name's Pete Marsh — you may remember — '

'I remember you,' Turner said.

Marsh's grey eyes held a steely glitter.

'I need a horse and a gun,' he said flatly. 'I've got some unfinished business to attend to.'

'Let it wait,' Turner advised. 'You're in no condition for anything. Sit down before yuh fall down, and I'll get you some food. I'll admit to being a mite curious how yuh came to get yourself in such a mess, though.'

Marsh started a grin and found it painful on his face.

'I'll tell yuh when I've eaten.'

He perched himself on the edge of

the bed and rolled a cigarette. The tobacco soothed him while he waited for the meal to arrive. He studied the doctor in the meantime.

Turner was tall and gangling, dressed in black. He had a long jaw and a beaky nose, and his Adam's apple bobbed up and down behind a starched, loose-fitting collar.

The meal arrived, steak and mash, apple fritters and black coffee laced with brandy. Marsh didn't speak till he'd finished eating, then leaned back in his chair, sighing contentedly.

'I feel fit enough now, doc. Tell me, no bones broken?'

Turner shook his head, lighting a cheroot.

'No. Surface damage only, but I'd still advise yuh taking it easy for a day or two.'

'And let them hombres get clean away? Not me, doc! If I can sit a horse and hold a gun, I'll be moving on.'

Marsh told the doctor what had occurred at the shack.

'It's happened before,' the doctor said, waving tobacco smoke from his eyes. 'South side of the valley is no longer safe for honest folk, not since Dyson and Hammond split up.'

'The sheriff scared or something?'

Turner looked carefully at Marsh.

'You ought to know better than to ask a fool question like that. Or maybe five years away from Gunsmoke Valley is longer than five years in it. You forgetting the sort of man Hammond is? And that the nearest law office is at Blue Forks, forty odd mile away? Hammond still thinks he's boss in these parts, 'cause he settled first. He won't allow any law but his own, and the sheriff stays away.'

Marsh grunted.

'Seems that times have changed. What's happened?'

'There was a row between Hammond and Dyson — remember him?' Marsh nodded. Turner went on: 'Dyson took his men south of the river. Hammond's pinned down north side, and there's

23

open war between them. Rustling and shooting's the order of the day,' Turner spat. 'One day someone's a-going to plug Dyson, and a lot of folk will be happier.'

Marsh sat quiet, remembering. Dyson had been in with Hammond, his right-hand man. He'd never liked Dyson, an effeminate man with cunning in his eyes; the opposite of Roger Hammond, who was a proud, hardhitting rancher. He said casually:

'How's Grace?'

Doc Turner squinted hard at Marsh and rubbed the side of his beaky nose.

'I'm beginning to get the idea of yore coming back,' he said softly. 'Sure, Grace is all right. A fine-looking gal, straight and proud like her dad, and she ain't picked a husband yet. I reckon it'll take a good man to tame her, and I'm wishing yuh luck — '

Marsh said: 'What's Hammond doing, letting Dyson play gunman?'

Turner shrugged.

'I'm not saying anything against

Roger Hammond — he's got his own troubles. I'll let you find out for yourself, when yuh meet him. You'll find him changed. He's an old man now, and his health ain't good. I keep telling him he ought to be in bed, but he doesn't take any notice of me. If you're a friend of the family, you'll try to get him to rest up and leave the fighting to others. Between ourselves, I don't expect him to live much longer.'

Marsh thought that over. It seemed to him he needed more information before he went against the men who had robbed him. Likely they were Dyson's men, and that meant moving against a big outfit. It was common-sense to ride out and meet Hammond first, to see how the land lay. And that would give him the chance to see Grace again.

He said: 'Step down to the bank with me, doc. I had some money transferred to River Bend before I set out; it'll be waiting for me, but I lost my papers of identification along with everything else

25

last night. If you say you remember me from the old days, that'll be good enough.'

Turner grinned.

'Glad to oblige. My fee's twenty dollars, and I'm mighty glad to have a patient aiming to settle up. Most folk say they can't afford to pay.'

Marsh and the doctor walked along the boardwalk to the bank. Marsh got some curious stares, but no one spoke except to pass the time of day with Doc Turner. The bank manager made no difficulty over drawing from his account, once Turner had identified him, and Marsh walked out with his pockets stuffed with greenbacks. He paid off the doctor, thanked him, and went shopping.

After the way Red had beat him up, Marsh needed a new outfit of clothes. He bought a thick flannel shirt and a slicker and Stetson, and called in at the gunsmith's.

'I want a long-barrelled Colt .45 and a Winchester rifle and shells — and I'll pay cash.' He put down his money and inspected the stock. 'I'll need a waist-belt and holster, too.'

Behind the shop was a long, narrow yard. Marsh picked up a tin can and tossed it high. He used the Colt, hitting the can four out of a six times. The gun had drift. He tried another, and was satisfied.

'Nice shooting!' the gunsmith said. 'I wouldn't like to get in a fight with you.'

'There'll be others thinking that before long,' Marsh replied, and slipped the Colt in its holster.

He paid the gunsmith, placed the rifle in the crook of his arm, and made his way to the stables. Joe Brett said:

'Hi, Pete! Something more I can do for yuh?'

Marsh nodded.

'The doc told me how yuh helped. Thanks! Now I want a horse, a good one with speed and stamina. You got something I can see?'

'Sure! Step inside. I've a nice sorrel yuh might take a fancy to. The boss ain't around, but it'll be all right to sell.'

27

Brett led the way into the stables, indicated the sorrel, and stood back while Marsh inspected the horse. Marsh took a liking to the sorrel right away. The horse was an ugly brute with a wild light in its eyes. It was young and hardy, of Indian stock, Marsh judged.

He said briefly: 'I'll take him, Joe. Name yore price, and throw in a saddle and halter — and add ten per cent for yourself.'

Brett shook his head.

'I ain't adding nothing. What kind of a man d'yuh take me for? I don't need paying to help a man in trouble — for my money, you can decimate some of the skunks holding out at the south end of the valley.'

'I was figuring on doing just that,' Marsh drawled.

He paid cash for the sorrel, mounted, and rode out of town, crossing the river by a wooden bridge. North of River Bend, he let the sorrel have its head; the horse travelled fast, effortlessly, hoofs thudding rhythmically, head craned forward and tail lashing. Marsh grinned; he'd picked a good mount, one he could rely on.

After a time he checked the sorrel's mad gallop and brought the horse under control. He swung westward, heading for the Hammond ranch. The ground was hard, lightly covered with a mantle of snow, brown grass showing through in patches. The few trees were bare of leaves, and the air was sharp, the wind edged like a knife. The sun was a red ball, dimmed by a grey sky and heavy banks of snow cloud.

He saw no sign of the vast cattle herd that Hammond kept, but crossed a trail showing where steers had run. That surprised Marsh, he'd have thought that the herd would be kept bunched near the ranch, for easy feeding in the hard winter. Then he remembered about the rustling . . .

Ahead, far distant on the trail, the long, jagged line of the plateau rose stark against the skyline. The prairie swept on in rolling dunes; Hammond's place, sheltered by close-growing pines and snug-set in a deep hollow, was still out of sight.

Marsh eased his pace as hoof-beats sounded. Riders were coming his way, from the north — Hammond's riders, with maybe the rancher among them. He spotted them as they swung up from a dip, five men bunched close together. He pulled in, waiting for them to reach him.

They came at the gallop, spreading out a little, reining in to form a half-circle about him. Roger Hammond was not present. The leader of the group trotted up to Marsh; he had a gun in his hand and a hard look in his eyes.

He said: 'All right, stranger, point yore hands at the sky and don't try any tricks!'

Marsh sat quite still, holding the sorrel's reins loosely in his hands. He made no move to raise his arms.

'Get 'em up! You hear me?' rapped the other man.

Marsh nodded slowly.

'Sure I hear yuh,' he said. 'I was wondering whether to let daylight through yuh, or leave it to Hammond. He picks strange riders these days.'

His words had a sharp edge and the man with the gun flushed.

'You'll stick yore hands in the air pronto, or I'll drop yuh!'

Marsh's face made a frosty smile. He was thinking this man was a blusterer, with little to back his words; Marsh had lived with men who used guns automatically — and he didn't doubt that he could shoot first, even though his own Colt was still holstered.

Another of the riders spoke: 'I reckon you're making a mistake, Fingle. This hombre doesn't look like a rustler.'

Fingle, the man with the gun in his hand, snapped: 'He's a rustler all right. Get yore rope ready, Lefty. No need to take him back to the ranch — we'll string him up now!'

Marsh stared at Fingle.

'You riding for Hammond?' he asked bluntly.

Fingle smiled unpleasantly. He was young, about twenty-five, and had fair — almost yellow — hair. He had a slender body and eyes that seemed to crawl over Marsh's face.

'Sure,' he said. 'We ride for Hammond. I'm his foreman. That make you any happier?'

Marsh didn't like the set-up. Fingle was just itching to hang him — and the other riders, though reluctant, would be bound to back up their foreman.

He said: 'There was a time when Hammond would have thrown an hombre of yore sort plumb in the river. I reckon he must be real sick to promote you foreman!'

Fingle choked, raising his gun. He snarled: 'Get that rope over a branch, Lefty! I'm sure going to lynch this rustler.'

Marsh looked round the half-circle of Hammond's men. They weren't happy about it at all and Marsh didn't blame them. Fingle would be a bad foreman, harsh, and too ready to use his power.

The man addressed as Lefty was running a lariat through his hands and staring down at the ground.

Not one of the four Hammond riders had drawn a gun on him — and that told Marsh how little faith they had in their foreman. Fingle would be the sort to get himself promoted over the heads of better men; he would be disliked, a jumped-up coyote always taking the boss's side against the men. Hammond must have been crazy to make Fingle foreman.

The rider who had spoken before was looking hard at Marsh. He said: 'Seems we've met before, fellar, but I can't seem to remember yore name.'

'Pete Marsh. I was around here five years ago. Hammond didn't allow lynching parties then — '

Fingle snarled: 'You dirty, lying rustler! You never met Roger Hammond in yore life, and you ain't going to now. I'm putting a rope round your neck and hanging yuh from the nearest tree.'

Marsh smiled bleakly.

'Better men than you have tried it! Listen to me for a moment. I came into this valley yesterday and ran into three tough hombres — I reckon the marks are still plain on me. Likely they're the rustlers you want, and I'll be as glad to get my hands on them as you. Suppose we ride to the ranch and see Hammond?'

Fingle sneered. 'A likely story,' but he was shaken by Marsh's casual sureness.

'I remember yuh now, Pete,' said the man who had spoken for Marsh. 'He's all right, Fingle. Hammond knows him, and he ain't riding for Dyson.'

Marsh said, 'Thanks,' and looked at him gratefully. The man was an old-timer, short and grizzled, with lank grey hair and blue eyes. He wore a battered Stetson and a slicker draped tightly about his thin frame.

Fingle snapped: 'That's what you say, Carey. Me, I ain't so sure. This hombre could still be in with the rustlers, and if he is — '

Marsh said coolly: 'I am content to

34

let Hammond settle it. I was on my way to see him when you butted in. I'll sure mention to him he has a foreman too handy with a rope — let's go, Fingle!'

The foreman kept his gun levelled.

'All right, Marsh. You ride ahead and don't try to make a break for it or I'll shoot yuh down.' He turned to the other riders. 'You carry on and see where them cattle went. Get moving now.'

Carey and Lefty with the other two Hammond riders moved off south, towards the river, following the tracks of the stolen herd. Marsh set his sorrel in motion, continuing on his way to the Hammond ranch. Fingle came up behind him, his Colt menacing Marsh's back.

Fingle said: 'Go on, try to break away. Go on, just try it — I'd love to pump yuh full of lead!'

3

Roger Hammond

Pete Marsh ran his sorrel at a fast trot, thinking how much things had changed in Gunsmoke Valley. He'd thought he had finished with gun-law and was returning to peace and quiet, to settle down to a steady life. Instead, within hours of his return, he had been beaten up and robbed, nearly lynched, and now —

Fingle rode behind him, gun ready for the death shot. Marsh knew the foreman was rattled. He'd made a mistake and wouldn't like news of it to reach Hammond's ears; so he'd got rid of his riders and was all set to kill — it would be easy enough for him to say that Marsh had tried to escape . . .

Pete Marsh smiled grimly. Fingle was going to get a surprise. He reined in the sorrel with abrupt sharpness, stopping dead. Fingle, coming up behind, nearly collided with him — and Marsh twisted in the saddle and grabbed his gun-arm at the elbow joint. His free hand smashed down on Fingle's wrist in a chopping movement, striking the revolver from his hand.

Fingle yelped in surprise and pain, and Marsh deftly caught the gun and turned it on the foreman.

'Now,' Marsh drawled, 'you can ride ahead and I'll carry the shooting-iron. I don't enjoy having a trigger-happy hombre like you having the drop on me. Get moving — Hammond will sure be pleased at the way yuh bring in a rustler!'

Fingle cursed bitterly.

'Damn you, Marsh,' he cried out. 'I'll see you swing for this!'

Marsh leaned across and whipped Fingle's mount to sudden movement. The horse bolted. Fingle almost came out of the saddle; he stopped swearing and trying to get at Marsh in his frantic need to stay on the runaway. Marsh galloped after him, laughing. He had the upper hand now and Fingle wouldn't bother him before they reached the ranch-house.

The foreman got his mount under control and Marsh jogged along a few yards behind him. Fingle looked round, looked into the muzzle of his own gun, and didn't start anything. He'd had enough and was beginning to realise he had jumped the wrong man. Marsh was a hard hombre and Fingle was more than a little scared.

They rode the remaining miles to the Hammond ranch at an easy pace and in complete silence. The ground sloped downward, thickly grassed and clear of snow. The pines were grouped like gaunt sentinels to one side of the layout of barns and corrals. A cinder patio surrounded the two-storey house and the only sign of life was some off-key singing from the punchers' bunkhouse. The cook preparing chow, Marsh surmised.

He slid from the saddle, still keeping his gun trained on Fingle, and called:

'Anyone home?'

Fingle climbed out of his saddle and stood looking from Marsh to the house. It was dawning on him that Marsh really knew the Hammonds, that he was going to look a fool in front of his boss.

'Look here, Marsh,' he began, 'if I've made a mistake — '

He stopped as the door of the house opened and a girl came on to the porch.

Peter Marsh caught his breath. Grace Hammond had been seventeen when he left Gunsmoke Valley and, even then, she had been lovely, with the promise of greater beauty to come. That promise had been fulfilled. At twenty-two, she was a woman of mature beauty, slim and graceful, with wide, dark eyes set in the smooth oval of her face. Her hair, which had been short and curly, was now an undulating wave of rich brown.

She came down the steps, her eyes on Marsh, a slow recognition coming to light them. She wore a plain dress that left her shoulders bare, and her skin was sun-kissed a golden colour.

She said, with a warmth in her voice: 'Peter — Pete Marsh! It's good to see you again. I thought you'd never come back, and I did want — '

She was looking at him closely.

'You've changed, Pete. You've grown hard. There are lines about your mouth and your eyes are cold.'

Marsh smiled, the strong lines of his jaw softening.

'You've changed, too, Grace. You've grown into a woman. Before, you were the loveliest girl in the valley . . . now you're the loveliest girl in all the world!'

She laughed softly, but her eyes were dancing and Marsh knew that he'd pleased her. Then she became aware of the foreman, and the gun in Marsh's hand. Her expression altered.

She said: 'What's the trouble, Pete?'

Marsh nodded at Fingle.

'Yore foreman tried to convince himself I was a rustler, and was all for stringing me up to the nearest tree, without so much as a trial. I had to unconvince him.'

He unloaded the shells from Fingle's Colt and spilled them on the ground, then tossed the empty gun at the foreman. Fingle caught it and stuck it through his belt.

Grace Hammond said angrily: 'You fool, Fingle! I've known Pete Marsh all my life. Dad will have something to say when he hears about this.'

Her tone was one of sharp rebuke and Fingle's face reddened.

He said: 'How was I to know? It's a safe bet any strangers in the valley are rustlers, and he was on our land, so — '

'So you tried to lynch an innocent man?' the girl snapped.

Fingle breathed hard.

'Listen, Grace — '

'Miss Hammond, to you!'

Fingle turned away, scowling.

'I'm going to speak to your father. I'm not convinced Marsh isn't in with the rustlers. It's mighty odd he should come back after five years . . . and maybe Roger Hammond will think the same!'

He moved up the steps and into the house. The door swung shut behind him. Grace Hammond looked speculatively at Marsh.

'Just why did you come back, Pete?' she asked.

Marsh was a simple, direct-thinking man. He said:

'You know why, Grace — to ask yuh to marry me. Will you?'

When the girl did not reply, he went on:

'Five years ago, I asked yuh the same question, and you laughed at me. You said yuh couldn't take a mere cowhand seriously, that you'd only consider a wealthy land-owner. Well, I'm that now, I have money in the bank and a ranch in Wyoming. I'm coming back to yuh as my own boss, a man who can give you what yuh want. And I'm asking now . . . will you marry me?'

He waited for her answer, outwardly calm, silently praying she would not ask the question he dare not answer. How had he got his money? It was because of Grace he had gone outside the law and was now a wanted man. But that was something he did not intend she should ever find out.

Grace Hammond spoke in a low voice.

'I must have seemed a spoilt child five years ago, Pete. I didn't deserve your love. But I've changed, you must know that. Your money isn't a passport to marriage. Perhaps you still love me, but I'm not sure of my own feelings — five years is a long time.'

She paused, hesitated, then said:

'I did love you, Pete. I knew that as soon as you went away. I had a feeling of emptiness — I cried at night, when there was no one to see. Now, I'm not sure if I can love you. I need time to find out. My father's a sick man, and there's trouble in the valley, so, you see, I can't leave him.'

She was watching him all the time, seeing his broad shoulders, the way he carried himself, the hardness of him.

She said: 'Dad needs help. Will you stay and fight alongside him?'

Marsh said simply: 'I'll do anything you say, Grace. Now I'd better see yore dad, before Fingle gets him convinced I've been running off his cattle.'

She led him into the house, to a large, pleasantly furnished room, where Roger Hammond sat listening to his foreman. Fingle shut up abruptly at their entrance.

Hammond rose, and said: 'Hallo, Pete, I reckon Grace is glad to see yuh again. I am, too — for her sake. Fingle, yuh can get out now. Get after them cattle and don't make any more mistakes.'

Fingle scowled at Marsh and left the room. Marsh studied Grace's father, and was shocked that five years should make so much difference to a man. He was thinner, the colour gone from his cheeks, and his hand shook as Marsh grasped it. His hair had whitened, his moustache, too. Marsh remembered the doctor's words: 'He's a sick man, and ought to be in bed.'

But Hammond still had the fighting spirit in him; his body was weak, but his courage was undaunted. He would be on his feet, fighting to the last to protect his interests.

'Fingle's a fool,' Roger Hammond declared. 'I must have been crazy, the day I made him foreman. You, Marsh, you've got the build of a real man. You looking for a job?'

Marsh shook his head.

'I can meet yuh on equal ground now, Mr Hammond. I own my own outfit.'

Hammond said: 'Where?'

'Wyoming.'

Hammond shot him a keen glance.

'And you're figuring on marrying Grace and taking her away from Gunsmoke Valley. Waal, perhaps that's best.'

He looked suddenly old and tired, and began to tremble.

Grace took his arm.

'Sit down, Dad. You must rest — you know what the doctor said. And you know I'll never leave you. Pete is going to stay and help us.'

Hammond snorted: 'Damn sawbones — thinks he knows how I feel, better than I do myself!'

But he sat down and let Grace place a cushion behind his head.

'So you're going to stay in the valley, Pete? From the marks on yore face, I judge you've already had a run-in with the scum polluting south side.'

Marsh rolled himself a cigarette, and lit it. He blew a smoke ring, nodding.

'Three hombres beat me up and robbed me. A red-haired giant with freckles, a skinny runt, and a man with a wart on his nose and wearing clothes so tight he almost burst them. I sure aim to meet those three again.'

Hammond was silent a moment, thinking over Marsh's descriptions. He shook his head.

'No, I don't know them. Must be three new ones — looks like Dyson is importing more roughnecks for the showdown.'

He looked at his daughter, and added:

'Grace, I want you to leave us now. There are things I have to talk over with Pete.'

The girl rose.

'All right, Dad. But don't go tiring yourself.'

She left them. Hammond came straight to the point.

'I'm going to tell yuh certain things I don't want Grace to know. Yuh got that?' Marsh nodded, waiting. Hammond went on:

'I'm getting old, Pete, with maybe not long to live — and I don't want Grace to suffer for the things I've done. You know me; I'm a proud man, hard. I've built an empire in Gunsmoke Valley and Grace will inherit. Waal, I wasn't always honest in my methods. I knew what I wanted, and went after it by any means that came to hand. I can see, now, that I did wrong — but the past

47

can't be wiped out. So I have to try to put things right.'

Marsh did not interrupt; he sat down, drawing on his cigarette, listening.

Hammond said: 'I'm not making excuses. I went outside the law. I hired men who'd take orders without asking questions; gunmen, rustlers, thieves. I took what I wanted with guns to back my play — I took over this valley and built an empire and made the laws myself. There were killings. My herd grew on rustled cattle. No small outfit dare stand against my gunmen. You see how it is, Pete? You see why I don't want Grace to find out about my past?'

Marsh nodded.

'And now?' he asked. 'Dyson has double-crossed yuh?'

A brightness shone in Hammond's eyes, the cold glitter of hatred.

'Dyson handled the gunmen for me — then he got ideas about taking over himself. He saw I was getting old, that Grace would get the ranch, and he'd be

48

out of it. So he tried to kill me! He failed, but took his men south and set up headquarters there. He rustles my cattle as it suits him, and Fingle and the men I have left aren't tough enough to stand up to him.'

Marsh crushed out his cigarette.

Hammond said: 'It's getting worse, and, what I want to know is — what's going to happen to Grace when I'm gone? I've got to settle this fast, and the only way is to drive Dyson and his killers out of the valley. And I can't go to the sheriff for help.'

Marsh drawled: 'If yuh fail, it's Grace who pays for the things you've done.'

Roger Hammond came out of his chair, stiff and proud.

'I won't fail, Pete. I'll beat them if it kills me — but I'd like to have yuh on my payroll. I'd like just one man who can stand up and fight!'

Marsh said dryly: 'Thanks!'

Hammond was studying him closely.

'I don't make mistakes, Pete. I'm a good judge of men. I don't know what's happened to yuh in the past five years, and you don't have to tell me — but I can see that you're hard, that yuh don't scare easy. And I have a notion you're a fast man with a gun.'

He sat down again, his eyes still on Marsh's powerful body and strong features.

'You love Grace, don't yuh? That's why you came back . . . Waal, I'm giving you the chance to help her when she needs help most. Gunsmoke Valley must be cleaned up. Will you come in with me and finish Dyson and his gang?'

Marsh didn't have to think about it; he knew what he was going to do. He said:

'I'll look after Dyson for yuh.'

Hammond smiled a little.

'I feel better knowing that. You'll look after Grace if anything happens to me. And she doesn't have to hear what I've just told yuh.'

Marsh said: 'She won't hear it from me, Mr Hammond — but don't you think it would be a good idea if she left the valley for a time? There's apt to be a lot of shooting before this is all done.'

'That's hard on an old man, Pete. If she leaves now, I may never see her again.' Hammond thought about it, and sighed. 'You're right, of course — she should go. Gunsmoke Valley is no place for a girl when we go after Dyson's outfit, but I reckon you'll have a helluva job convincing her of that. She's fighting blood in her, my blood — and I'm damned proud of it, too. Call her back now.'

Marsh left his seat and walked to the door, opened it and called: 'Grace.'

Grace Hammond came swiftly, smiled at Marsh and took her place at her father's side.

'Well,' she said calmly, 'is it settled? Is Pete fighting with us?'

Hammond touched her hand, his eyes bright.

'He is!'

She looked at Marsh, and said: 'I'm glad.'

Hammond brushed his moustache very carefully with his hand, staring hard at the floor. He spoke quietly:

'Grace, both Pete and I agree yuh ought to clear out for a while — just till we've rid the valley of Dyson and his vultures. I reckon that won't take long —'

The girl glanced coldly at Marsh.

'I suppose this is your idea? Well, I won't go!' She held herself proudly, her jaw rock-hard, her eyes flinty. 'I won't leave dad, and that's flat.'

Marsh said easily: 'It would be best, Grace. I figure there's going to be a lot of rough stuff.'

She said: 'I'm staying!'

Roger Hammond chuckled.

'What did I tell yuh, Pete — she's got my blood in her veins. You're sure saddled with a woman in this war!'

Marsh didn't like it, but one look at Grace told him it was no use protesting. She had her mind made up and no one was going to change it. Suddenly he found himself admiring her.

'I guess I never really expected anything else,' he said, and laughed.

Hammond and Grace watched him.

'What yuh got to laugh at?' Roger Hammond demanded.

Marsh didn't answer. He thought it ironical that he had returned to Gunsmoke Valley, expecting to settle down peacefully. He was an outlaw, fighting a gang to save Grace from finding out that her father was no better . . .

'To-night,' he said slowly, 'I'll be riding south!'

4

The Message

The hour was late when Pete Marsh set out to pay a return visit to the shack on south side of Gunsmoke Valley. He travelled light and rode fast, thinking to strike swiftly and then withdraw. He rode alone under the dark, cloud-filled sky, his hand resting on the smooth stock of his rifle. There was a wind, sharp-edged and keening through the trees, driving powdery snow into his face.

Marsh headed east to by-pass the town of River Bend, then turned his sorrel southward. The horse's hoofs drummed rhythmically on the hard ground; the animal's breath made a ghostly mist in the cold air; the motion of the saddle was familiar and strangely comforting to a man who had ridden

54

with outlaws and been hunted by a posse. Sometimes the moon would break through the banks of cloud, silhouetting a lone pine or the distant line of plateau with a pale glow.

He reached the river and sent his mount down the frosted bank, into the swirling water. The sorrel swam strongly, reaching the far bank and climbing up between scrub and aspen. Marsh rode carefully now, his ears pricked for the sound of danger, his gun-hand tense. He was in enemy territory, wary but not afraid.

There were landmarks to guide him, a faint trail, a half-felled cottonwood, a rocky cleft where rattlesnakes made their home. He crossed the prairie and came to the stream between the pines, and followed the rough trail leading to the shack. Even before he came in sight of the lighted window, he knew that someone was there; the wind brought him the scent of a log fire. Marsh had a feeling it would be Red and his two cronies, and was glad. He remembered the beating they had given him and wanted his revenge.

He slipped from the saddle and left the sorrel's reins trailing the ground, then, rifle in hand, moved up to the shack. He paused behind the shelter of a pine trunk, fifteen yards from the door, and whistled. From behind the shack came a frenzied stamping of hoofs, a shrill whinnying — his horse, Starlight, was there and recognised his call. Starlight must be well-tethered, Marsh thought, or the gelding would have come running.

The door of the shack opened abruptly, swinging back on its hinges, and a big man stood silhouetted against the yellow oil-light. Marsh recognised the ugly, freckled face, the bull-neck and tawdry red hair.

He called: 'Red. This is Pete Marsh. I told yuh I'd come back to settle the score — and here I am!'

Red mouthed an oath, darted side-ways and flattened himself against the shadowed wall of the hut. He shouted to the man inside:

'Put that light out. We've got company!'

Marsh waited. He was in no hurry to start the fight. The three roughnecks had made a mistake of thinking themselves safe; they had misjudged his character, believing he would not return. So they had stayed on at the shack, not knowing the kind of man Marsh was — the kind of man who made up his mind to a course of action and ploughed ahead regardless of the opposition. They were going to learn the hard way.

The lamp went out, leaving only pale moonlight to show the hut, bare and stark against the trees. A window creaked open and a man climbed through; thick-set and fleshy, he wore tight-fitting clothes. A bullet hit the woodwork close by his face.

Marsh laughed, calling:

'Wart-nose — I told yuh what happened to horse-thieves. I've a rope handy and there's plenty of trees. You can pick the one you'd like to swing from.'

A shot ripped through the dark silence of the night. The slug thudded into the tree behind which Marsh waited. He held his fire. It had not been Red or Wart-nose who had shot at him; that meant the skinny runt was still around — and Marsh had to be sure there were no more than these three to deal with. They couldn't guess he was alone, of course, which gave him an advantage. They would think he had come back with a posse and would be wondering whether to fight it out or make a run for freedom. Marsh intended them to go on wondering.

He had fixed the third man's position now, low-down behind the water-barrel. Marsh brought up his rifle and let fire; his shot drove into the woodwork close enough to the skinny runt's head to make him grunt and wriggle further under cover.

Marsh said: 'You boys going to throw down yore guns?'

No voice answered. Away to Marsh's left, a twig cracked. Marsh brought round his rifle and triggered lead at the spot. Movement ceased. Marsh guessed it was Red, trying to work round his flank; he wondered if Wart-nose were trying to do the same on the other side. He peered into the darkness, seeing nothing, and cursed the clouds that blotted out the moon; he would need to wait before he could be sure.

But one thing was certain in his mind; he had only the three men to deal with. If there had been others, they would be rushing him instead of skulking in the background. Marsh said:

'I'm going to get you boys!'

A shot came, a stabbing red flame from his right. Marsh marked down the place but did not return fire. Instead, he wedged his rifle upright in a cleft in the pine and draped his stetson over the muzzle; when moonlight came, his opponent would have a target, but it wouldn't be Pete Marsh. He drew his

Colt and snaked forward on his belly, moving silently to fresh cover. Then he waited for the action to start.

Long seconds elapsed, tense and hushed. The wind made the only sound between the trees. The darkness shrouded hunter and hunted. Death waited for the moon to show —

It came suddenly, clouds, sliding from the pale disc in the night sky. A cold silver light flooded the glade; and three shots echoed together, ripping Marsh's stetson from its perch. Marsh came to his feet, startled by Red's closeness. The big man was no more than ten paces away, his back to him.

Marsh said: 'I'm over here, Red.'

Red turned, snarling with rage at being tricked. His gun-arm came up. Their guns roared almost simultaneously, but Marsh was a shade faster. His slug tore into Red's chest, stopped the big man in his tracks and ruined his aim. Marsh felt the lead wing past him and knew that Red had fired his last.

A slug nicked his cheek, drawing

blood. Marsh wheeled about, facing Wart-nose, and triggered lead fast. The fleshy man sagged, the colour fading from his face. He hit the ground and rolled over. Marsh thought grimly: Two down and one to go!

The moon disappeared behind a cloud, leaving him in darkness. There was absolute silence. Marsh dropped to one knee, resting his Colt steady, waiting for the skinny runt to make a move. He felt around for a stone, closed his hand on a loose flint and tossed it sideways. The stone hit bracken with a tearing sound and crimson flame stabbed the gloom. Marsh's gun roared noisily, aiming for the flash.

Somewhere in the dark a man cried out, cursed bitterly and crashed to the ground. He lay there, moaning quietly. Marsh waited, thinking it might be a trick; he kept quite still with his gun levelled. A voice came:

'Marsh, don't shoot! My arm's broken and I'm in pain. Don't shoot!'

Still Marsh did not move. He kept his

Colt pointing in the direction from which the voice came and waited for the moon to show. After a few minutes, the darkness gave way to a silver glow and he saw the skinny runt lying on the ground and holding his arm. Marsh advanced.

'Throw your gun away and stand up!' he ordered.

The wounded man called: 'For pity's sake, I'm hurt. I need help!'

Marsh stood over him, gun levelled, his grey eyes steely. His tone of voice was harsh, almost grating.

'You held my arms while Red bashed my face in. I'll give yuh the same kind of pity. On yore feet!'

The skinny runt scrambled upright; one arm hung limply at his side, the blood trickling down his leg. His face was white and screwed up with pain. Marsh saw then that he was pulling no trick; the bullet had shattered his wrist.

Marsh said: 'I ought to kill you, but I need you to run an errand. First, I want my money-belt and guns back. And if you've harmed Starlight you can start praying!'

The agony of his shattered arm forced tears to the skinny runt's eyes. He cried out:

'Can't you do something for my arm? The pain — the pain — '

Marsh smiled coldly.

'Quit bawling, fellar! I've a heart of stone when it comes to dealing with hombres of yore kind. Get into the hut!'

Sweating with pain, the man obeyed. Marsh stooped over the bodies of Red and the fleshy man. Both were dead. Marsh felt no pity for them; both men had been outlaws and murderers. The west would be a cleaner place without them.

He lit the oil lamp, and said: 'What's your name?'

'Webber,' the skinny runt replied sulkily. 'Your money-belt's in the corner. We hadn't split it up yet. Now, for mercy's sake, fix my arm, will yuh?'

Marsh ignored him, checked that the money in his belt was intact, and strapped it round his chest. His guns were still where he had left them. He thrust the muzzles through his waist-belt.

'All right,' he said coldly. 'Outside. Walk in front of me, round to the stable. And remember, I'd as soon shoot you as not!'

Starlight was unharmed. The sable gelding with the white markings whinnied for pleasure at sight of him and nuzzled his hand. Marsh untethered the horse and saddled up.

'Which is yore horse, Webber?'

'The grey.'

Webber looked badly scared. His eyes were frightened and he was shaking; he realised he could expect no mercy from Pete Marsh. A man used to dealing out violence, he had no stomach for facing someone as violent as himself.

Marsh turned loose the grey, and said:

'Get on, Webber! Get out of here pronto. Go and tell Dyson I'm coming after him, then keep riding. If I meet yuh again, I'll kill you on sight! Understand?'

Webber nodded, tight-lipped. He climbed awkwardly on to the back of his horse and raked the animal's flanks with his spurs. The grey leapt forward, carrying Webber out of sight.

Marsh watched him go, holstered his Colt and stood a moment surveying the deserted glade. It would not do to linger; Dyson's men might be nearer than he thought. He turned the dead men's horses loose and returned to the shack. He spilled oil on the floor and smashed the burning lamp on the boards. Angry red flames licked hungrily at the dry timber; black smoke eddied up. Marsh hurried outside; the shack would be ashes in a short time. Dyson's men would need to find another hide-out.

He collected his rifle and stetson, mounted Starlight and took the sorrel in tow. The dead men he left where they lay. Other outlaws would see their bodies and know that Pete Marsh was a man to be reckoned with. He started back for the river, and the Hammond ranch beyond.

There was a calm recklessness to his manner, a calculated hardness. Tonight he had avenged himself and carried the fight to the enemy. He wondered briefly how Dyson would receive his message — and anticipated the bloodshed to come.

★ ★ ★

Webber rode his horse hard, without looking back, using the slack of the reins as a whip and digging his spurs into the animal's flanks. He rode as if the devil were after him, crashing through scrub and chaparral in a direct course for Dyson's ranch. The sweat of fear was on his brow and he ignored the pain of his shattered wrist, now swollen to twice its normal size, before he could be sure that Marsh was not at his heels. A man like Marsh would be crazy enough to follow him into Dyson's camp — might even be using him for that very purpose — and Webber had no wish to meet up with Pete Marsh again.

He left the pine belt and headed across the open prairie, to the south-west. The clouds had thinned out and the moon was bright. The miles flashed by, and presently he came to slightly rising ground flanked by red-ochre bluffs. Beyond the rise there was a sharp fall leading to Dyson's ranch.

Webber rode down the trail at a gallop, wanting only to deliver his message and get out of the country. He had been scared and was running because that was the sort of man he was.

Moonlight shone on the roof of the big house, on the wooden shacks and corrals and hay-barns. The layout formed a triangle, with all the buildings inside high timber walls. There were lights showing in the windows of the big house; Dyson was a man who worked at night and slept by day. The place looked more like a fortress than a ranch-house.

Webber slowed his mount as he approached the pool of light surrounding the open gateway. Beyond the rim of light, he knew, would be armed guards. A voice called out:

'Who is it?'

'Webber. I've got to see Dyson in a hurry!'

He rode slowly into the circle of light and waited while a man came closer and took a good look at his face. Webber couldn't see the second man, but knew he would be there, finger on the trigger of a rifle. The first guard said:

'All right, Webber. Yuh can ride in.'

Webber flicked the reins, urging his horse forward. He rode up the cinder path to the front of the big house, slid out of the saddle and hitched his grey to the wooden rail before the veranda. The house was built of wood, two-storeyed, with an ornate façade; the white-walled portico had massive columns decorated in gilt, and there were roses painted on the walls in red and yellow and blue.

Webber went up the steps and pushed open the door. A lighted corridor led through a wide hall to a room where men's voices sounded. A stairway wound upwards from the hall and there were hanging drapes and thick carpets. Dyson was a man who liked luxury.

Webber's arm hung limp, throbbing with pain; his hand was matted with the blood, the side of his chaparejos stained. He stood in the doorway and looked at the room where Claude Dyson lived. It was a large room, comfortable, with richly-coloured Navajo blankets on the floor and solid furniture upholstered in red leather with carved legs. Again, there were hanging drapes on the walls, and the whole room bore an air of obvious wealth.

There were two men present, and both turned to study Webber as he said:

'Dyson, I've a message for yuh!'

Claude Dyson leaned back in his

chair, a cruel smile on his lips.

'You seem to have got hurt, Webber,' he said smoothly. 'Can I offer you a drink? Brandy, perhaps, or a good whisky? I only stock the best.'

He was a slim man with curly black hair and sideboards, but the cunning in his eyes belied his effeminate appearance. He looked a dandy, and dressed and acted the part. But Webber was not fooled. He knew that Dyson was dangerous, a snake who would strike from cover and boast of his duplicity.

He answered: 'I'm not staying. Pete Marsh shot Red and Clem. He said he's coming after you, and told me to leave the valley.'

Dyson was briefly amazed, then laughed. He was an elegant figure in bottle-green trousers, tucked into the tops of polished riding boots, and a short crimson jacket. He wore two guns, the handles inlaid with pearl and silver.

'Who,' he asked, 'is Pete Marsh? And do you really mean to tell me that one man beat the three of you?'

Webber moistened his lips with the tip of his tongue.

'There's no need to use that tone of voice, Dyson. This Marsh is a killer. You want to watch out. Me, I'm getting out of Gunsmoke Valley pronto!'

Dyson pulled a red leather box from his pocket, flicked open the lid and took out a pinch of snuff. He inhaled deeply through each nostril in turn, returned the snuff-box to his pocket and dusted himself down with a white silk handkerchief.

'You're really leaving us, Webber? You needn't you know. I'll take care of Marsh for you.'

Webber shivered.

'He said he'd kill me on sight. And he would! I'm leaving!'

'You're a yellow-livered runt!' said the man with Dyson. 'You'd run if a woman slapped yore face!'

Webber looked at the speaker, a solidly built man with a bald head and scarred face. His nose was an eagle's

71

beak and his guns were heavy-bore Colts. This was Stoat, Dyson's second-in-command.

Webber said: 'You got no right to speak like that, Stoat. This Marsh is dangerous! You'll find out. Didn't he shoot Red and Clem?' He held up his injured arm. 'And look what he did to me — '

'If I'd been there,' Stoat said slowly, 'I'd have killed this Marsh. I wouldn't have run away like a scared kid!'

Webber's shattered wrist began to throb again. He nursed it to his chest, stared from Stoat to Dyson, then said:

'I've delivered his message and now I'm leaving. He's coming after you, Dyson. When he finds yuh, you'll understand why I'm getting out!'

He hurried from the room. The West was a large place and he intended searching out a corner where Peter Marsh would never set eyes on him again.

Claude Dyson moved to the window and looked out. He saw Webber mount his horse and go through the gateway at a gallop.

He drawled: 'Something really scared that little runt. I think I'd like to know something about this tough hombre, Marsh. See what you can find out, Stoat!'

The bald man hitched up his gun-belt.

'If I run into Marsh,' he said, 'all you'll need to know is where he's buried!'

Dyson nodded, and Stoat went out.

'It sounds as if Marsh might be a good man to have on my pay-roll,' Dyson mused to himself. 'Certainly, Hammond cannot be allowed to hire him.'

He took the snuff again and flicked the breast of his crimson jacket with his handkerchief. He spoke aloud.

'Either Marsh throws in with me, or he must die!'

Pleased with that decision, Claude Dyson settled comfortably in a chair to wait for Stoat's report.

5

Rivals

The morning sky was grey with cloud. The snow still held off, but a chill wind swept the grassland and moaned through the pine branches. Pete Marsh was up as soon as light came through his window; he shaved and dressed and went down to breakfast. A privileged guest, he dined with Hammond and Grace, not in the bunkhouse.

Roger Hammond said eagerly: 'Well, Pete, how'd it go last night? I see yuh got your horse back.'

Marsh glanced sideways at Grace. Though normally a blunt man, he had no desire to talk of killing in front of the girl. He answered briefly:

'Those three bad hombres won't worry you, Mr Hammond. I gave them an even break and a chance to throw

74

down their guns. I shot two. The third man carried a message to Dyson; after that, he'll be leaving the country.'

Hammond's eyes gleamed.

'You hear that, Grace? We've a real man fighting for us at last. That's the way I'd have handled it in the old days, but I'm getting past it now. Good work, Pete. I reckon this'll stir up that ornery skunk, Dyson!'

Grace said: 'You mustn't get excited, Father. You know it's bad for your heart. You weren't hurt, Pete?'

Marsh shook his head, eating steadily.

Hammond wiped bacon grease off his moustache and said: 'What yuh going to do next, Pete?'

Marsh finished eating and pushed the empty plate away from him.

'I figure on making a tour of your range, Mr Hammond. I want to see the cattle, and the men, and decide how best to defend ourselves if an all-out attack comes. Maybe I'll ride into town to see how many folk there will fight with us.'

Grace frowned.

'River Bend folk are just fine at sitting on the fence,' she said. 'You won't find many willing to risk their necks against Dyson.'

Marsh drawled: 'That so? Seems like I'll have to stir them up then.'

Roger Hammond explained: 'Dyson's outfit ride openly into town. So far, there's been no trouble between them and my men. You see, we both need stores, and River Bend is the only town for forty miles. The merchants sell to both of us. And look the other way if we arrive in town at the same time. It's a sort of no-man's land, by unspoken agreement.'

Marsh rolled himself a cigarette and lit up. He blew a stream of smoke across the table.

'You mean that Fingle sees Dyson in town and does nothing?'

'Fingle!' Hammond snorted. 'I've wished a dozen times I had never made him foreman. He's a good puncher, but bad with the men and no gunfighter.

But I won't go back on my word, so he stays foreman. You'll have to get on with him as best you can, Pete.'

Marsh nodded. Fingle didn't worry him half as much as this casual acceptance of River Bend as a no-man's land. He said deliberately:

'I shall tell Dyson to stay away from River Bend; any of his men I find there will be used as targets for shooting practice. That will force the townsfolk to take sides, for they can hardly ignore flying lead. I figure they'll come over on our side, and that will cut off Dyson's supplies.'

Hammond shot him a searching glance.

'You got the guns to back that kind of play?'

Marsh's grey eyes held a steely smile; the lines tightened about his mouth. He touched the butts of his Colts.

'I can take care of it, Mr Hammond.'

Grace said: 'I'll saddle my horse, Pete. You'll need someone to show you the full extent of the range, and the men are busy.'

She kissed her father and left them. Hammond watched Marsh intently for a while. Finally, he spoke.

'Keep Grace out of this, Pete. I don't want her hurt. You're a hard man, used to fighting alone. This time you've got a woman at your side. Don't ever forget that.'

Marsh stubbed out his cigarette butt and rose from the table.

'I'll watch out for her,' he said curtly, and went outside to the stables.

He was crossing the cinder patio when he saw Grace and Fingle, and a frown came to his face. The slim, fair-haired foreman had the girl against a railing of the horse corral; his arms were round her, and he was trying to kiss her. Grace struggled to break free.

Marsh quickened his pace, closed the gap between himself and the foreman, and reached out his long arms. He grabbed Fingle's shirt and dragged him away from Grace, held him a moment, then threw him bodily at the corral. Fingle winced with pain, and cried out.

Marsh didn't look at the girl, his whole attention was on Fingle.

'Being foreman doesn't give yuh privileges of that kind,' he said harshly. 'Let me find yuh bothering Miss Hammond again and I'll break every bone in yore body. Stay away from her, fellar!'

Fingle was hurt and angry. His hand dropped to his gun, but he did not draw. The expression on Marsh's face warned him he was a dead man if he tried that. Fear flickered through his eyes; he gulped and tried to get a grip on himself.

'Damn you, Marsh, mind your own business! Grace and I have an under-standing — '

Marsh slapped him across the mouth.

'Shut up, Fingle — and get out of my sight! You're paid to look after cattle, nothing else.'

The foreman backed away, appealing to the girl.

'Grace; tell him that me and you are riding into town.'

Grace Hammond looked at him with contempt. She answered shortly:

'Not this morning, Fingle. You'd best go about your business now.'

Fingle scowled and turned away. Marsh looked at Grace, who said nothing — she mounted her horse and waited for him to join her. Marsh saddled Starlight, and together they rode away from the ranch-house.

Grace let her horse run over the grass; her rich brown hair streamed out behind, and her slim body was curved with the motion of her mount. Marsh looked at her and thought her beautiful; she had a proud bearing which she inherited from her father. Her skin was smooth and sun-kissed, and her riding clothes were cut to show the fullness of her womanly figure. She remained calm and unruffled after Fingle's handling.

Marsh drew alongside her, and asked:

'Fingle bother yuh often, Grace?'

She flashed him a quick look, and answered:

'No — not often. Forget him, Pete. He wants to marry me, but there's nothing between us, I swear it. But I'm the only woman here, and — well, a girl likes to have admirers. I suppose it's my own fault; I should have slapped him down earlier.'

Marsh said no more; he'd been away five years, and it was natural that other men should take an interest in a pretty girl. He remembered how Grace had been spoilt and used to having her own way; she'd probably considered Fingle an amusing diversion till he got serious. Now she was sorry she'd let him get familiar.

So the foreman wanted to marry Grace . . . that meant he had a rival. Marsh decided that Fingle would bear watching; he might give trouble in the future.

Grace rode east, parallel to the northern rim of the plateau.

'Our main herd is wintering in Broad Hollow — there's a creek feeding the river, and good grass. It's sheltered

81

from the wind, too.'

It was a ten-mile ride to Broad Hollow, and the steers made a black mass stretching to the horizon. There was one wooden shack, used by out-riders, at the south end.

'Too far from the ranch and not sufficiently well-protected from rustlers,' Marsh said critically. 'Your riders can't do much in the open. They need cover if they're to fight off Dyson's outfit.'

'We've lost a good many head of cattle,' Grace admitted, 'but what can we do? The rangeland nearer the ranch is eaten out, and it's a hard winter. We must put the stock before rustlers.'

Marsh stared across the miles of empty prairie; the river, and Dyson's territory, was too close.

'The cattle will have to be moved,' he said, and rode down the slope to the shack.

He recognised the old-timer with grey hair and blue eyes who came up to meet them; it was the man who had spoken for him when Fingle had wanted a lynching party.

Marsh said: 'Hallo, Carey! I'm riding with Hammond against Dyson. How many men you got who can handle a gun?'

Carey smiled happily.

'At last!' he breathed. 'So Hammond's got a fighting man at last! You've a good outfit, Marsh, nine men — maybe not all gunfighters, but all willing to try. We're fed up running from Dyson. All we want is a leader, and I reckon you're him. Fingle still foreman?' he added casually.

Marsh nodded.

'Fingle will run the herd; I'm handling the fighting. Right now I want these cattle moved. We're too close to the river to make a stand. Get your men together and drive the cattle north; I want them penned behind the ranch-house. There's a basin under the plateau, with gullies leading into the cliffs. We'll rig a wire fence to keep the steers in and feed 'em hay.'

Carey looked a question at Grace.

'It's all right, Carey,' the girl said. 'Do as Pete says.'

The old-timer scratched his grey hairs.

'The idea's good,' he drawled, 'but it's going to mean a lot of work — and feeding stuff's expensive.'

'It'll only be a temporary measure,' Marsh said. 'With the cattle safe, I'll be free to deal with Dyson. Then the herd can move back here. Get the men together and make a start.'

Carey rode off to collect the punchers and tell them what was wanted. They got behind the steers and began to drive them north, slowly at first, concentrating on the leaders. The cattle were reluctant to move, and the men had to use their stock-whips. Marsh took a hand at moving the herd, Grace, too. The girl was a true-born Westerner, at home in the saddle, and she worked as hard as any of the men.

Carey came riding by.

'I smell trouble, Pete,' the old-timer

said. 'Fingle's headed this way, and he ain't going to like yore giving orders.'

Marsh drawled: 'I reckon he'll just have to get used to it then!'

Carey moved away as the foreman came abreast of Marsh and Grace Hammond. Fingle snapped:

'What the hell d'yuh think you're playing at Marsh? This is the only winter feeding ground we have; the cattle must stay in Broad Hollow.'

Patiently Marsh explained what he was doing. Red anger spots showed in the foreman's cheeks; he turned to the girl.

'I'd have thought you would have more sense than to take orders from a gunfighter, Miss Hammond. This move is crazy — the cattle will starve. Your father won't approve of this . . . And I'm off to tell him what's happening!'

Fingle wheeled his horse round and galloped off in the direction of the ranch-house. Grace looked at Marsh, smiling faintly.

'I'd better go after him,' she said.

'Dad must know your side of it, too.'

Marsh nodded.

'And rustle up some grub for the boys. This job is going to take time, all day and most of the night. I'm going to keep 'em moving till every steer is well out of Dyson's reach. We'll eat in the saddle. You might see about posts and wire while you're at the ranch — we'll need several miles of it.'

Grace rode away, and Marsh returned to the cattle drive. Nine men were not many to herd the thousands of cattle Hammond owned, and the beasts didn't like the hard ground or the biting wind. The dust rose in great choking clouds. The air was filled with the cows' bellowing. The ground shook with the stamping of hoofs.

Marsh rode in and out of the stragglers, beating their leathery flanks with his Stetson, shouting at them, using Starlight's shoulders to turn the obstinate ones. Carey and the punchers had the cattle bunched in a long line, a hundred horns wide, and were forcing them north, away from Broad Hollow. Despite the bitterness of winter, it was hot work. Marsh took a pull at his water canteen and adjusted the neckerchief over his nostrils. The dust hung like a grey pall, visible for miles.

Marsh sought out Carey again. He said:

'Dyson will see our dust and know we're moving the herd. Likely he'll attack. Pick three or four men who can shoot straight, and have them keep to the rear. I'll be there myself.'

Carey wiped dust out of his eyes.

'I'll attend to it, Pete, but Dyson ain't the sort to show himself in daylight. If he comes, it'll be after dark.'

'We'll be ready for him!' Marsh said grimly.

At noon Grace joined them with the chuck-wagon. Fingle was back, too; the foreman did not speak to Marsh, but got on with the job of driving the herd. He kept to a flank distant from Marsh.

Grace said: 'Dad approves of the move — you're in charge, Pete.'

Marsh smiled, imagining that Fingle had got little sympathy from Roger Hammond. He signalled two of the riders.

'Stop off at the wagon and get some eats,' he told them. 'Only two of yuh drop out at a time. We must keep the cattle moving.'

Grace took her turn with the steers, but Marsh saw that she kept well forward. He didn't want her around when Dyson struck. Dusk came early, a gathering greyness low down on the horizon; black clouds rolled overhead. The sun set, the last rays showing blood-red through the haze. Darkness blotted out everything.

Marsh dropped to the rear, leaving the drive to Fingle and the punchers. He patrolled the tail of the herd, watching for the riders from south side. A cold wind had sprung up, carrying with it a few flakes of snow; the rumble of hoofs sounded eerily in the dark. The grass was trampled flat, leaving bare, hard earth, and he could no longer see the dust, only smell it.

Presently, the moon showed through the cloud. Marsh tensed; this would be what Dyson waited for. The darkness to hide him — yet enough light to see by. The attack came with a suddenness that told Marsh the rustlers had been following behind, waiting only for the moon to show.

He saw a dozen riders galloping towards the herd. They were spread out in a long line and carried guns in their hands. Marsh fired his rifle into the air as a signal; Carey and four other men dropped back to engage the rustlers.

Marsh placed his rifle across the saddle-bow and headed for Dyson's outfit. Ahead of him, gun flashes made bright red lances in the gloom — Carey had made first contact. Marsh sighted his Winchester and pumped lead with methodical precision. He was too far off to hit anyone, but he wanted to show Dyson that he had a fight on his hands. If the rustlers knew they had been seen, they might sheer off, and Marsh wanted to avoid a pitched battle if he could. Cattle were queer critters, easily alarmed; if the gunfire came too close, they might stampede.

Dyson's men were obviously surprised to meet with resistance. They hesitated in their headlong gallop, scattered, splitting up and racing to left and right along the flanks of the slowly moving steers. The cattle at the rear pressed forward, bellowing wildly. Marsh had one clear view of a rustler, shot quickly, and dropped the man. The horse bolted south, dragging the dead man along the ground till his foot jerked from the stirrup.

Marsh's jaw set in a grim smile. First blood to us, he thought, and pushed fresh cartridges into the empty magazine of his gun. Staccato shooting started away on his left; he wheeled Starlight in an arc and rode fast for the sound of the engagement. Carey was on foot, his horse dead beside him. There was a milling crowd of riders beside him, rustlers and Hammond's men shooting it out. The moon, dodging behind clouds, made it difficult to tell friend from foe.

Marsh rode straight into the crowd, gun raised. He saw a bearded face, half-masked, and pushed his gun at the face, triggering lead. The rustler shrieked and covered his eyes with his hands as he fell; a frightened horse stamped on him as it crashed past.

Carey shouted over the noise of his Colt: 'They're cutting out the beef!'

Marsh turned again, used his rope to catch a riderless horse for Carey, and emptied his rifle at four Dyson riders busy heading stragglers southward. The rustlers were pulling out. They'd had enough of the fight and were running for it, taking a score of cows with them.

Carey, mounted again, said: 'We going after them, Pete?'

Marsh holstered his guns and shook his head.

'Not this time. We must secure the herd first — the showdown with Dyson can wait. Anyone hurt?'

Carey rode round his men, and reported:

'Smith took a flesh wound, nothing serious. We dropped three of them. Not bad, considering they had the advantage.'

'Not bad,' Marsh agreed. He listened to the pounding of the cattle's hoofs. They were on the run, northward, but hadn't stampeded; Fingle and his men would be able to control them. 'Not bad, Carey,' he drawled, 'but next time we must do better.'

Grace Hammond rode up, the anxiety leaving her face when she saw that Marsh was unhurt.

'How'd it go, Pete?' she asked.

'We lost about twenty head — and got three of them. I reckon they've had a lesson they won't forget.'

'Dad will be pleased,' Grace said.

Smith came up, his shirt torn and bloodstained. He was grinning broadly, despite his wound.

'Mighty nice to have yuh with us, Marsh,' he drawled. 'I always did figure those rats would run if a real man showed up!'

Marsh rolled himself a cigarette.

'Better get that wound fixed, Smith. We've work to do, and I don't reckon on carrying any man. When Dyson comes into the open, I'll need every man who can use a gun — so get that arm fixed, pronto!'

6

A Shot From Cover

After the herd had been driven into the basin behind the Hammond ranch, Pete Marsh divided the men into two shifts, allowing each shift four hours sleep. Even though a lot of hard work remained and time was short, he did not make the mistake of driving his men till they dropped from exhaustion. Food and rest were vital if they were to combat Dyson efficiently.

Marsh took his rest period with the second shift, rising late the same morning. He breakfasted, and rode out to see how the fencing was going. Fingle was in charge and, although the men were working fast, it would be several days before the whole area was penned off; in the meantime, he had to arrange for a regular arrival of feeding stuff from River Bend.

He called in at the ranch on his way to town, and found Grace hitching a four-horse team to the largest of the Hammond wagons. She was dressed in denims and an old shirt, with her hair tied at the nape of her neck; she looked as brisk and businesslike as she was lovely.

'Someone has to fetch the cattle feed from town,' she said calmly, 'and none of the men can be spared for it. I can drive a wagon as well as anyone so I'm doing the job. Any objections?'

'I reckon you can do it,' Marsh replied. 'I'll ride in with yuh.'

He used a long rope to hitch Starlight to the rear of the wagon, then climbed up beside Grace. He took the reins from her and pushed off the brake.

'You rest easy,' he said. 'It'll be a hard drive back with the wagon loaded, and I shan't be with yuh.'

He drove the wagon out of the yard and headed the team south.

'Going looking for trouble?' the girl

asked, staring straight ahead.

'I just want to start things moving in River Bend,' Marsh said. 'It's time folks there realised they can't sit on the fence for ever. Dyson's got to be cleared out of town — if that means trouble, I'll be ready for it.'

He glanced down at the boards under Grace's feet; she had placed a rifle there, ready to hand.

'You stick to freighting hay,' he told her. 'If there's gunplay, stay out of it — that's my end of the job.'

'Sure, Pete; anything you say.'

Marsh glanced sharply at her; her acquiescence had been too easy. He repeated:

'Stay out of the fighting, Grace.'

He whipped the team to greater speed and the wagon lurched clumsily on the rough trail. The wind was cold, the sky grey; bare earth showed through patches of stunted grass and a thin layer of snow still clung to the pine branches. Neither Marsh nor Grace spoke much on the drive. Marsh was thinking how different his return had been from the peace he had expected — and it did not please him that he was forced to appear as a gunfighter before her. He wondered how much of his past she had guessed — and what she really thought of him.

He knew that he loved this girl sitting beside him, and respected her. She had the guts it took to live rough without complaining; she would make any man a fine wife. But could she love him if she knew he had lived with a gun in his hand, wanted by the law? Her expression revealed nothing of her thoughts.

The miles passed and the town of River Bend showed on the horizon. Marsh drove over the wooden bridge and turned into Main Street, pulling up in front of the feed store. He handed Grace down from the wagon, and they went into the store.

'Howdy, Miss Hammond,' the storeman said. 'How's your dad?'

'The same as usual — too stubborn to take any notice of the doctor's advice.' Grace Hammond came directly to the point of her business. 'I want to buy your entire stock of feeding stuff, every ounce you have. I'll write a cheque now, and ship it as we need it. Will that be all right with you?'

The storeman looked startled.

'That's an unusual order, Miss Hammond, but I reckon it'll be all right. Mind you, I wouldn't do it for anyone else. Some trouble at the ranch?'

'No trouble we can't take care of ourselves,' Grace replied calmly. 'Will you get your men to load the first instalment now? My wagon's outside.'

'Sure, miss.'

The storeman went to the back of the counter and opened a door. He shouted into the yard, telling his men to start loading the wagon. When he came back he looked at Marsh, and said:

'Heard there was some shooting on the Hammond range last night. Heard that three of Dyson's men didn't return. You Pete Marsh?'

Marsh nodded. The storeman paused a moment studying him, and Grace.

'Pete is riding for us,' the girl said coolly. 'He has my father's approval, and that goes for everything he does, too. Do you expect us to sit by and let rustlers take off our cattle without a fight?'

The storeman seemed uneasy.

'Dyson's a pretty big man now, Miss Hammond. Shooting's only going to make more trouble. I'm a peaceable man myself, and — '

'What you mean is that you're afraid to stand against Dyson,' Marsh interrupted coldly. 'The man's a rustler, an outlaw, a killer — yet you merchants watch him walk down Main Street and do nothing. You take his money — and ours — and sit on the fence, hoping no one points a gun yore way. Waal, I'm changing all that. I'm warning Dyson to stay out of River Bend or have a fight on his hands . . . And when the lead starts flying you'll have to take sides. You siding with a rustler or with Hammond?'

The storeman looked scared.

'We don't want trouble here, Mr Marsh. We — '

Marsh cut him short.

'Trouble's coming, whether you like it or not. You just have to make up yore mind which side to fight on — ours or Dyson's.'

Grace added: 'We lost a score of cattle last night. I was there myself. I saw the riders — and they work for Dyson.'

The storeman ignored her, turning angrily on Marsh.

'You talk big, Marsh — let's see how yuh act. Dyson and a couple of his men are in town now.'

Grace said, 'Oh!' and watched Marsh carefully.

Pete Marsh hitched up his gun-belt and squared his shoulders. His voice had a hardness in it.

'Stay out of this, Grace,' he said, and walked through the door.

Main Street was quiet. A few women were shopping. A couple of men shot dice on the boardwalk. Someone was leading a horse to the smithy.

Marsh walked slowly up the centre of the wide dirt street. He had tension in him; his fingers were curled very close to the butts of his Colts. His grey eyes were sharp, stabbing at faces, searching for Dyson. There was no fear in him, only a cold awareness. He was a blunt, direct-acting man. Dyson was his enemy — therefore he sought out Dyson.

Three men came from a saloon down the street, moving towards horses that were hitched to the wooden railing. The man in front wore a crimson jacket and bottle-green trousers. Marsh recognised the effeminate figure with curly black hair, and called:

'Dyson! I want you!'

Claude Dyson turned, facing him, waiting. The two men with him stepped apart, one to each side and a little behind their leader; their hands rested on revolver butts. Marsh walked forward and stopped before Dyson; he looked into cunning, snake-like eyes, and saw the cruel smile of a killer.

'Well,' Dyson said easily, 'what is it? You're Marsh, I suppose?'

'I'm Marsh . . . '

Dyson studied him thoughtfully, took snuff with a nonchalant air, and dusted himself down with a silk handkerchief. Still acting the dandy, Marsh thought; five years hasn't changed your character any.

'I'm glad we've met,' Dyson said calmly. 'It saves me the trouble of seeking you out. I've something to say myself.'

Marsh stood with legs apart, braced for action, his brain ice-cool and his hands steady. They had Main Street to themselves, the residents of River Bend had taken cover.

Marsh said loudly: 'Tell yore watchdogs to shift their hands away from those guns — before I blow their fingers off!'

'You think you could?' Dyson appeared interested. 'You've already proved that you're a good man with a gun, Marsh, but don't push your luck too far. You're not dealing with Webber now — I'm not the sort to run.'

Marsh said doggedly: 'Tell them to take their hands away from their guns.'

Dyson shrugged.

'I don't want gunplay unless it's forced on me. It's in my own interest to keep the peace in town. Relax, boys! Marsh only wants to talk.'

Marsh took a quick look at Dyson's men. One was bald with a scarred face and a beak of a nose; he looked tough. The other man was long and thin; he wore thigh-high riding-boots with unusually long spurs. Both men shifted their hands at Dyson's command.

Dyson took snuff again. He said coolly:

'I want you on my side, Marsh. Come over to me and I'll pay yuh double what Hammond's offered you. You'll find it to your advantage to be on the winning side. I've seen your sort before — you're a professional gunman, not Hammond's type. Throw in with me and you'll find we've a lot in common. I can overlook — '

Marsh interrupted: 'Save yore breath, Dyson! Hammond's not hiring me; he's a friend of mine, and I'm standing by him to the end. You can't buy me. Now listen to what I have to say — '

He pushed out his jaw, feeling the lines harden round his mouth. His eyes stared into Dyson's, freezing him.

'Get out of town — and stay out! From now on the sight of any of yore men in River Bend will be the signal to throw lead! My riders have orders to use yuh for target practice, and I'll be leading 'em! Now get on your hosses, and ride!'

Dyson flushed. The bald-headed man growled menacingly. The thin man moved his shoulders, crooked his arms for a quick draw.

'Get going!' Marsh said flatly.

Dyson seemed to have difficulty in

speaking. He choked on his words.

'No one talks that way to me, Marsh! For that I'm going to kill you!'

Somewhere close by a window shattered with the noisy tinkling of glass. The barrel of a rifle poked through, directed at Dyson. A voice said clearly:

'The first hombre to go for his gun is a dead skunk!'

Dyson started, taken by surprise. The bald man rumbled:

'This is a trap! Let's get the hell out of here!'

The three men, cursing, backed away, their gaze divided between Pete Marsh and the rifle across the street. They unhitched their horses and mounted. Dyson shouted: 'I'll be back to kill you, Marsh!' And spurred his horse to a gallop. They disappeared southward, out of town.

Marsh stood watching them go, then turned towards the broken window. Grace Hammond came from the building, a rifle in her hands and a satisfied expression on her face.

Marsh said: 'I told yuh to keep out of it, Grace. If those hombres had jumped their guns, you'd have likely got hurt, and I promised your father that I'd look after you.'

Grace tucked the rifle under her arm and stood with her hands on her hips.

'Pete Marsh,' she said calmly, 'you're a fool! Only a fool would be stupid enough to face three killers the way you did. If I hadn't been behind that rifle you'd be a dead man now.'

'Maybe, Grace — maybe not. But then Dyson would be dead as well. In future, stick to driving the wagon and leave the fighting to men.'

The girl tossed her head defiantly.

'It's my fight, too. If anything happens to dad, the ranch will come to me.'

Marsh walked back to the wagon, now loaded, and unhitched Starlight. He tethered his horse to the rail outside a saloon and helped Grace aboard the wagon.

'Get back to the ranch,' he told her, 'and stay there. I'll be back as soon as I've tested out local opinion. Maybe some folk in River Bend will come out against Dyson now that I've shown we mean business.'

Grace took up the reins.

'Look after yourself, Pete. Dyson meant what he said, and I don't like the idea of being made a widow before we even get married.'

Marsh looked at her, wondering.

'You mean that, Grace? You want to marry me?'

'Pete Marsh, you're an even bigger fool than I thought! Of course I want to marry you!' She picked up her driving-whip. 'What you've just done is the bravest thing I've ever seen. It was magnificent! Dad will be proud . . . and I love you for it.'

She cracked the whip and jerked on the reins, driving the wagon away before Marsh could say a word. He stared after her, his lips softening in a smile, a sudden happiness surging through him.

107

People started to gather on Main Street, talking excitedly. Doc Turner came up, tall and gangling, his Adam's apple bobbing agitatedly over his collar.

'That was fine, Pete, just fine. Time somebody told that skunk Dyson where he gets off. Come into the saloon — I want to buy yuh a drink.'

He took Marsh's arm and walked him through the swing doors, up to the counter. There was quite a crowd there already, and men parted eagerly to let them through. Joe Brett shouted:

'I'm with yuh, Pete — we'll drive Dyson and his outfit clear out of the valley!'

Turner spilled some coins on the counter.

'Fill 'em up, barman,' he called. 'This round's on me. We're drinking to freedom — and the man who's going to lead us. Pete Marsh!'

Somebody said: 'If Dyson doesn't get him first.'

Marsh lit a cigarette, drawling: 'I'll take my chance when he makes his stand.'

He finished his drink and listened to the comment in the bar. It seemed to him that River Bend was divided; about half the town were glad of the chance of getting rid of Claude Dyson; the other half were scared of being caught in a gun-battle. No one had a good word to say for Dyson.

Marsh had learnt what he wanted to know — River Bend would back him against the rustlers on south side if it came to open war. He pushed his way to the door. Doc Turner caught up with him and held his arm.

'Pete,' he said, 'watch yourself from now on. Dyson's no fool. He'll see what yore game is — forcing him out of town, this way. River Bend's on your side now, but for how long? If Dyson puts a slug through yuh, the town will go to sleep again. Look after yourself, 'cause Dyson will try to kill you for sure.'

Marsh said grimly: 'I'll be waiting for him.'

Turner shook his head.

'Not that way. It'll be a shot in the back when he does try, and you won't see Claude Dyson. It'll be one of his men, Stoat, likely — he was the bald-headed hombre you just met. Dyson thinks a lot of him for that sort of job.'

Marsh freed Starlight and climbed into the saddle.

'Doc,' he said quietly, 'the way I've been living the past five years, I've developed eyes in the back of my head!'

He nudged his horse to motion and rode down Main Street, across the bridge and taking the trail for the Hammond ranch. The clouds had shifted a little and wintry sunlight peeped through, bathing the prairie in cold light. The wind was chill and he rode along at a brisk pace.

Marsh wasn't looking at the countryside; his thoughts were with Grace Hammond — she loved him and wanted to marry him. Marsh was feeling content, Dyson and his outfit far from his mind as he skirted a pine-belted bluff. The ground was rough and he swayed a little in the saddle — and it was this motion that saved his life.

The shot came without warning, a single whip-like crack from far off. Starlight reared. Marsh felt a stinging sensation in his head. Something wet and sticky ran down his face and his vision blurred. He felt the strength leave his arms, and slid sideways, falling from the saddle. He lay still on the ground, half-dazed — the gelding galloped off, circled, stood waiting at a distance.

There was complete silence for several minutes. Marsh fought off the blackness threatening to engulf him. He forced his eyes open, searching for the man who had ambushed him. He lay in the open, without cover, his rifle still in the scabbard on Starlight's saddle. He had only his Colts, and they were useless at long range.

The bluff was the only place his ambusher could be — and even that was a difficult distance for a rifle shot. Marsh thought grimly: Whoever it is has a high-powered gun fitted with telescopic sights — if I show sign of life, he'll finish me with another shot.

He kept his head motionless as he studied the pine trees. Light glinted on the metal barrel of a rifle, and Marsh had the man's position fixed. He waited. Perhaps the would-be killer would come closer, to make certain of his murder shot. If he did — Marsh's hand tensed, wanting to reach for the revolver at his waist. But he must not move —

His head throbbed and it was an effort to keep his eyes open. There was a chasm of darkness waiting to swallow him up if he relaxed for an instant. He wondered just how bad his wound was, and knew that he was lucky to be alive.

There was a movement amongst the pines. He saw a man come from behind the trees, mount a horse and ride swiftly away. Not bothering with me, Marsh thought; he's quite sure I'm dead. One day I'm going to surprise that hombre —

He raised his head for a better view of the rider heading south for the river. A bulky man, hatless. At that distance, Marsh couldn't see his face, but there was something familiar about his build. Just then the sun shone brightly for a few seconds — shone on the smooth surface of a man's bald head.

7

Dyson Makes a Deal

Ted Fingle, foreman at the Hammond ranch, was unhappy. Since Pete Marsh had returned to Gunsmoke Valley, he had lost a lot of power. Roger Hammond no longer relied on him — and Grace ignored him.

Fingle was young and unmarried and wanted to make Grace his own. He'd thought she was interested — till Pete Marsh returned. Now she treated him as if he were a leper. Her manner revealed the contempt in which she held him; her tongue carried sharp reproof. Fingle was irritated by his own failure to make Grace love him, and filled with bitter hatred for Marsh. The future he had built up for himself — owner of the Hammond range — as Grace's husband, was slipping from his grasp. He felt frustrated and discontent.

Even the 'punchers showed their preference for Marsh, obeying him with alacrity where they would take the foreman's commands only because he represented Roger Hammond. Hammond was a sick man and Fingle had been able to handle him without much trouble — and Grace had accepted his advances without demur. Now, with Marsh's return, all that was changed.

Fingle's handsome face darkened in a scowl; he wished Marsh dead. At that moment, Grace was fussing over Marsh, nursing him and waiting on him the way Fingle wanted her to wait on him. He wished that Dyson had killed Marsh in ambush, instead of only wounding him. Marsh had things too much his own way; he had saved the herd from the rustlers and organised the winter food-store. The fencing had been completed. River Bend looked like coming over to Hammond's side and, soon, Marsh would move against Dyson. Fingle could see that his days at the Hammond ranch were numbered, his chances with Grace gone — unless something happened to Marsh.

Fingle toyed with the butt of his gun, shivered, and gave up the idea. The notion of shooting it out with Marsh sent a shiver of fear through the man; and Fingle had no real guts when it came to a showdown.

He began to wish he had thrown in with Dyson when he'd had the chance. Dyson had offered him a job — but he'd turned it down, gambling on Grace and grabbing the Hammond range for his own. His plans were coming badly unstuck. Dyson wanted Marsh dead — so did Fingle, though for a different reason. And he was going to be a hard man to kill. Now, if they could set a trap —

The more Fingle thought about it, the more he liked the idea. Dyson was the man to help him, then Grace would fall to him. The seed of jealousy grew in Fingle, making him reckless. Yes, he would go to Dyson and make a bargain

— Marsh's life for Grace's safety. He didn't have to stay in Gunsmoke Valley; he could persuade Grace to sell out before Dyson stripped the range of every steer. They'd have money to start again, elsewhere.

Fingle made up his mind. He saddled his horse and left the ranch, riding south across the plains. With the thought of Grace and Marsh urging him on, he made fast time to the river, holding his mount to a gallop. He headed his horse into the water and swam across, climbing the opposite bank — but once over the river, his nerve failed him. He was on Dyson's land, and a Hammond rider could expect no mercy if he were caught by the rustlers.

Fingle slackened his pace, purpose wavering. He might get a slug between the eyes before he reached Dyson. They might not kill him at once, but play with him a little. Fingle shuddered; he was a man who could not stand physical pain. Almost, he turned back.

It was the thought of Grace that drove him on when courage failed. His desire for her swamped his fear. She was fire in his blood and he would not give her up. Marsh must die! He gritted his teeth and rode on, keeping well clear of the cattle trails. He moved through the pine belt, using all the cover he could find, and reached the bluff overlooking Dyson's fortress.

He paused, studying the layout, relieved that none of Dyson's men were between him and his goal. He had only to ride down the slope, into the patio and talk to Dyson; it was as simple as that. Fingle hesitated. There was fear in him. Dyson was a killer —

Fingle swore, ashamed of himself. If he were to get Grace, he must be bold. Marsh didn't hesitate when he went into action; Fingle imagined Grace watching him now — and spurred his horse forward. He arrived at the gateway and checked his mount hurriedly as a shot whined past his head.

A harsh voice demanded: 'Hold still,

Fingle. Release yore gun-belt and raise your hands high!'

Fingle said: 'I want to see Dyson, pronto.'

'You going to drop yore guns or do I let daylight through yuh?' the guard replied.

Fingle unbuckled his gun-belt and let it fall. The guard came up, revolver levelled. He retrieved the foreman's guns and drawled:

'Sticking your neck out, aren't yuh, Fingle? You reckoning on leaving here alive?'

Fingle sweated. He said hoarsely: 'Let me see Dyson.'

'Sure you'll see the boss.' The guard laughed. 'He'll be pleased to see Hammond's foreman! Get off yore horse.'

Fingle dismounted and stood waiting uneasily, while a second guard came up. The first man took charge of Fingle's horse.

'Take him up to the house, Slim,' he grunted, 'and watch him for tricks.'

Slim pushed the muzzle of a Colt into Fingle's back.

'I'll watch him closer than a dancing girl!' Slim said easily. 'And I'll sure drop him cold if he takes a step out of line. March, fellar; up to the big house. Dyson will want to deal with you, personally.'

Fingle walked quickly up the cinder path, trying not to think of the gun Slim held at his back. He mounted the steps between the heavy gilt columns on each side of the door and went into the house. Dyson and Stoat were talking together in a luxuriously furnished room.

'Visitor for yuh, boss,' Slim said laconically. 'Hammond's foreman just rode in as if he lived here. We've taken his guns.'

Claude Dyson, immaculate in green and crimson, lifted an eyebrow in surprise. Stoat pulled a gun and held it on the foreman.

Fingle said: 'I want to talk to you in private, Dyson. I can help you — and need your help.'

Dyson regarded him keenly, then smiled. It was a cold, snakelike smile, with no friendliness in it. He took a pinch of snuff.

'All right, Slim, you may go. Mr Fingle won't be any trouble.'

Slim left the room. Stoat growled:

'He'd better not be. I finished Marsh, and I'll do the same for him — with pleasure.'

Fingle glared at the bald man.

'You didn't kill Marsh,' he retorted. 'Your shot only grazed his head. He's sworn to get you, Stoat — '

Dyson cursed, rounding on the bald man.

'I told you not to make any mistake, Stoat. I've no use for failures. You told me — '

Stoat said: 'He's lying, boss. It's a trick. Sure I killed Marsh. I had him plumb in my sights and he hit the ground like a sack of potatoes. I couldn't have missed.'

'He fooled yuh,' Fingle answered. 'He

121

was only grazed, and lay doggo till you'd gone, then rode back to the ranch. Miss Hammond's been fussing over him like a broody hen, and he only got a scratch.'

'So,' Claude Dyson said softly, 'Marsh still lives! Why didn't you go down and finish him, Stoat? Those were my orders.'

The bald man rubbed his scarred jaw and glowered.

'I was a way off, and he didn't move. There might have been someone on the trail, so I got away pronto. Yuh said you didn't want anyone to know you were behind the killing.'

Fingle felt better; he was enjoying Stoat's discomfiture. He said:

'He recognized yuh, Stoat. That bald head of yours gave you away. He's coming after yuh . . . '

Stoat swore.

'I'll be ready for him, and this time I'll make certain!'

Dyson sat down.

'Put yore gun away, Stoat,' he said

easily. 'Mr Fingle's come to offer his help.' Smiling, he pushed a bottle and glass across his desk. 'Help yourself, Fingle — you look as if you need a stimulant. Tell me, how is the lovely Miss Hammond?'

Fingle poured himself a half tumbler of whisky and drank deep. He scowled.

'All Grace thinks of is Pete Marsh. Since he came back, I haven't had a chance with her. Damn him!'

Dyson made a sighing sound. A cunning light showed in his eyes.

'So,' he murmured, 'now we're getting to the motive for your visit. I've always known she was the reason you didn't throw in with me.'

Fingle snapped: 'Well, I am now! I want Marsh dead, and I can help you. As foreman, Marsh has to trust me. I can lead him into a trap for you. All I want is for you to leave Grace alone. She's mine.'

Stoat said in disgust: 'You're yellow, Fingle, streaked right down yore spine! You're in a position to finish Marsh any time yuh want. Why don't you shoot him?'

The foreman flushed crimson.

'I'm no gunman — and Marsh is. He's a killer if I ever set eyes on one. He won't be easy to kill.'

Dyson drawled: 'A bullet in the right place will kill any man, Marsh included. But your idea of a trap sounds good. It will make it easier. Tell me, how far do Hammond and his daughter trust this Marsh?'

Fingle laughed harshly.

'He's got 'em both eating out of his hand!'

Claude Dyson placed his fingertips together. He looked down at his desk, up at Fingle. He spoke softly, with the sibilance of a snake.

'And tell me, Fingle, how will Hammond and his daughter react when they learn that Marsh is wanted by the law?'

The foreman started.

'Is that true, Dyson? If it were true . . . why, Grace would turn against him — and Hammond would have to disown him!'

Claude Dyson laughed, helped himself to more snuff, and flicked at his jacket with a silk handkerchief.

'It's true enough, Fingle. One of the new men to join my band recognised him. During the past five years, Marsh has been hold-up man and rustler. He's wanted — and there's a price on his head.'

Fingle's eyes glistened. His breathing quickened; he clenched his hands. This was what he needed to know; the thing that would finish Marsh with Grace Hammond. He could hardly wait to tell her . . .

Dyson, apparently reading his mind, said: 'You'd better get back now. Tell Hammond what I've just told you. I'll be waiting to deal with Marsh when he rides out — alone.'

He nodded at Stoat.

'Escort Mr Fingle as far as the river. I wouldn't want him hurt while he's running my errand.'

Stoat pushed the foreman to the door.

'Get moving, hombre,' the bald-headed man grunted. 'I ain't wasting all day playing nursemaid to you!'

Fingle left the house and walked down the gravel path to the gate. Slim and the other guard viewed him with interest.

'Waal,' Slim drawled. 'If yuh ain't still breathing! The boss must have run out of lead. Yuh want a gun, or a rope, Stoat? Or maybe a branding iron?'

Stoat said curtly: 'Get his horse. We're riding.'

Fingle said: 'I'll have my guns, too.'

Slim looked questioningly at Stoat.

'Give him his guns,' Stoat growled. 'He ain't the guts to pull on me.'

Slim handed Fingle his gun-belt, and the foreman strapped it about his waist. He mounted his horse and waited while Stoat brought a brown mare from the corral. They rode out of the gate and made for the river.

Fingle was feeling relieved at getting

away from Dyson's ranch with a whole skin; all he wanted now was to get rid of the bald man. They did not speak on the ride, nor did they meet anyone. At the river, Stoat turned back; Fingle swam his horse to the north bank and set a straight course for the Hammond ranch.

He felt pleased with himself. Dyson had given him the ace card he needed. Marsh — wanted by the law! That was going to make Grace change her opinion about him. Yes, Marsh was finished at the Hammond ranch; and what might happen to him after that, Fingle neither knew nor cared.

Pete Marsh sat on a chair under the lean-to built against the outside wall of the Hammond house. He was out of the wind and had an oil-stove to warm him. He smoked a cigarette and cleaned his guns, pausing from time to time to look across the patio, to the grassland stretching clear to the horizon.

There was a bandage about his head

and his wound still bothered him a little. It was two days since Stoat had ambushed him; and for two days Grace had kept him in the house, insisting that he was not well enough to ride. Marsh loved Grace, and liked having her around, but two days' inactivity was beginning to pall. He was a man built for action, not sitting around waiting while there was work to be done.

He oiled the mechanism of a Colt, spun the chambers and loaded them. It was time, he decided, that he rode into River Bend, to prove to folk there that he could keep his word when he told Dyson to stay away. There was one man that Marsh hoped would not keep out of town, the bald-headed Stoat. Marsh dropped the Colt in its holster and stood up. For several minutes, he practised a fast draw. His face was grim-lined, his mind on the man he intended to kill.

He did not hear Grace approach. She stood by, silent, watching him. Finally, she spoke.

'I don't like to see you do that, Pete. You look like a killer, a man who shoots for the pleasure of killing. I know you have to go armed in the West, and fight when it's needed, but this — '

She gestured with her hand. Marsh dropped the gun into his holster, and said:

'I don't like it either, Grace. When I came back to the valley, I hoped to marry and settle down, to put gun-fighting behind me. It hasn't worked out — and never will until Dyson has been dealt with. Guns are all that outlaws understand. They have to be fought that way.'

He drew a deep breath, looking into the girl's dark eyes.

'I take no pleasure in killing, Grace, but sometimes it has to be done. It's the only way. Kill or be killed — and I don't intend to let Dyson take this range from yuh.'

Grace sighed, and changed the subject.

'I've brought you a hot drink,' she

129

said. 'How's your head, today?'

Marsh took the cup.

'I'm all right,' he said briefly. 'Just figuring on saddling Starlight and riding into River Bend. This sitting around doing nothing is getting me down.'

'I suppose — ' Grace Hammond began, and stopped.

A horseman was headed for the ranch, travelling fast. Marsh recognised the slim, fair-haired figure of the foreman.

'Fingle,' he said. 'Looks like more trouble.'

Grace stepped out to meet the foreman as he rode into the patio and dismounted. Marsh loaded another gun and slipped it in his holster. He was hidden by shadow and Fingle did not see him immediately. Roger Hammond came out of the house, to learn what had brought the foreman back in such a hurry.

Fingle looked pleased with himself. His walk had a swagger and his eyes gleamed. He was obviously excited about something.

Hammond demanded: 'Well, what is it? Why aren't yuh with the herd?'

'I've news for you,' Fingle blurted out, 'important news.' He looked at Grace. 'You'll need to hear this, too. It's about Marsh — he's an outlaw, and wanted by the law. There's a price on his head. D'you understand, now? Marsh is one of Dyson's breed, as I said at the beginning.'

Pete Marsh stepped into the open. He said quietly:

'Who told yuh that, Fingle?'

Fingle moved back, placing Hammond and Grace between himself and Marsh. His face was white. Somehow, he hadn't reckoned on Marsh being present when he made his speech. He was frightened, his lips dry.

'I — I heard it from a man,' he stammered. 'Someone who knew yuh before you came back here.'

Marsh smiled thinly. His one word was fired like a pistol shot.

'Who?'

Neither Roger Hammond nor Grace spoke; they watched both men intently. And Fingle knew he was alone — alone against Pete Marsh, the man he had branded gunman. He pulled himself together; he had to convince the Hammonds.

'It was Dyson told me,' he said. 'One of his men — '

Roger Hammond exploded: 'Dyson! You've been talking to that double-crossing skunk? You expect me to take his word against Marsh's? You fool — if I weren't a sick man I'd put yuh across my knee and thrash yuh!'

Fingle flushed, flustered. It seemed everything was going wrong for him. It had been a mistake to mention Dyson's name, he saw that now — Hammond's sympathy went straight away to Marsh.

Hammond said angrily: 'You're my paid foreman, Fingle — and you talk to Dyson, my sworn enemy. You — you — '

Grace took her father's arm.

'Quiet Dad,' she said calmly. 'You

mustn't get excited — it's not good for you. Pete; is this true?'

Marsh looked at her, and knew he could not lie. Hammond, white-haired and frail, was shaking.

He said: 'It's true, Grace. I am an outlaw, a wanted man.'

Hammond said: 'That doesn't matter, Pete. You're the man to fight Dyson — we need you. Yuh hear that, Grace? I'm backing Marsh. What d'you say to that?'

Grace's dark eyes met Marsh's grey ones. She said levelly, without hesitation:

'Whatever you've done in the past makes no difference now. Dad's right — we need you to fight Dyson. No one else can stand against him. You're a gunman — and we have to fight fire with fire.'

Marsh did not take his eyes off her.

'That's not what I want to hear, Grace.'

Her expression softened.

'This doesn't make any difference to

133

us, Pete. I love you, and will marry you when this is over.'

Marsh nodded, turning his attention to Fingle. The foreman did not see his hand move, but suddenly there was a gun pointing at him. Fingle shook with fear, licking his lips, whining.

'Grace, for mercy's sake — you wouldn't stand by and see murder done?'

Marsh said: 'Stay out of this, Grace.'

Roger Hammond pulled his daughter aside.

'He's yours, Pete. Deal with him as you will. A foreman who runs to Dyson is no man of mine.'

Marsh held his gun on Fingle. There was a fierce anger in him for what the foreman had done; he wanted to punish him — but he couldn't shoot with Grace standing there.

'Drop yore guns, Fingle,' he said coldly, 'and kick them away from you.'

Fingle obeyed. Marsh calmly unbuck-led his own gun-belt and handed it to the rancher.

'Now,' he said. 'Put up yore fists, Fingle — I'm going to thrash yuh within an inch of your life!'

Fingle had been shaken by Hammond's casual acceptance of his news. He had made a big mistake of banking on the rancher disowning a known outlaw — and he'd lost Grace. There was fury in him as well as fear. Fingle hurled himself forward, ripping punches to Marsh's head.

Pete Marsh staggered back, taken by surprise. The gun-wound in his head opened and sharp pain shot through him. He swung his arms wildly, connected with Fingle's jaw by chance, and drove him off. The foreman saw that he'd hurt Marsh and came back eagerly. If he could kill Marsh with his hands —

But Marsh wasn't waiting for the attack. There was a red mist before his eyes, and he stepped forward, arms going like pistons, slugging heavy blows to Fingle's body. Fingle tried again to get at Marsh's head, and found his blows warded off. A fist landed under his jaw, stopping him cold; another drove into his stomach, winding him; a third punch knocked him to the ground.

Marsh said: 'Get up. Get up and fight, damn yuh!'

The foreman rolled over, came to his knees and sprang for Marsh's legs. He brought Marsh to the ground and they wrestled in the dust, exchanging punches. Fingle used his boots, kicking Marsh in the chest. Marsh grabbed a handful of hair and jerked Fingle's head back, hurled his fist into the foreman's face. Blood ran from Fingle's nose; one eye puffed up. He broke free and scrambled to his feet.

Marsh came after him. Fingle was desperate — he leapt forward and caught at the bandage about Marsh's head, pulling down the white cotton over his eyes, blinding him. He hammered blows into Marsh's body and drove a knee into his groin. Marsh groaned, falling, pulling at the bandage to uncover his eyes. Fingle dropped on top of him, snarling like a wild animal and trying to get his hands round Marsh's throat.

Pete Marsh ripped the bandage from his head. His grey eyes blazed with anger. He got his arms round Fingle's waist, lifted him clear of the ground and threw him back. He was on his feet before Fingle, waiting for him to rise. The foreman came upright slowly; and Marsh went in, battering him to the ground.

Fingle crawled away, picked up a chunk of rock and hurled it at Marsh. It struck Marsh's thigh, numbing his leg — and Fingle saw his last chance. He jumped Marsh, gouging for his eyes with fingers clawed. Marsh went over backwards, gasping for air; they wrestled again on the ground. Marsh took one of Fingle's arms and bent it across his chest, exerting all his strength.

The foreman shrieked once, went limp, then began to blubber. With the desperation of an animal in pain, he tore his arm free and tried to run. His arm hung limp at his side. Marsh rolled over and reached out his arm; his hand closed about Fingle's ankle, and jerked. Fingle fell flat on his face.

Marsh stood up. He caught hold of Fingle by the slack of his shirt and scooped him up, slammed his fist into the foreman until he lost consciousness, then dropped him like a sack of waste.

Hammond said: 'That was some fight. I reckon Fingle's had that coming for a long time.'

Marsh filled a bucket with water at the pump. He carried the bucket over to Fingle's sprawling form and emptied it over him. The cold water roused Fingle. He sat up, groaning.

Marsh said: 'Get on yore horse, Fingle, and get out of here. If I see yuh in the valley again, I'll kill yuh for sure.'

Fingle got to his feet, swaying. He felt as if a stampede had run over him. Without a word, or a look at Grace, he moved for his horse. He climbed painfully into the saddle and rode out of the patio.

Hammond spat.

'And good riddance!'

Grace smiled faintly at Marsh.

'If only all our troubles could be settled as easily,' she said. 'I don't think we'll be seeing Fingle again.'

Marsh drawled: 'I'll settle things for yuh, Grace. Don't worry about Dyson.'

She answered: 'I wasn't thinking of Dyson; only of you. Come into the house and I'll bathe your head . . . '

8

Dyson's Prisoner

Next morning, Pete Marsh saddled Starlight for the ride to town. The wintery sky was overcast by cloud, low, heavy banks, threatening snow. The wind was cold. Marsh's head was clear — his fight with Fingle had served to tone him up — and he knew he had to settle things with Dyson soon. The cattle would have to be moved back to Broad Hollow if they were to survive the winter. Marsh frowned; somehow he had to force the River Bend fold to form a posse and move against the rustlers on south side.

Grace Hammond came from the house as he was about to leave the ranch, Marsh waited.

'It's dad,' she said. 'I talked with him again last night, about fetching the sheriff from Blue Forks. He wouldn't hear of it, and I can't understand why. I think it's time we had the law on our side. Do you know why he's so set against having the sheriff in Gunsmoke Valley?'

Marsh knew it was on account of Hammond's past, but he couldn't tell Grace that. She would be deeply hurt if she learnt how her father had built up his empire.

'Maybe it's because of me,' he said lightly. 'I'd be in an awkward position if the law came here.'

Grace shook her head.

'No, it's not that. The sheriff need never know about you, Pete, and dad has always been against bringing in the law, even before you returned to the valley.'

Marsh remained silent, and Grace went on:

'It didn't matter before, when dad was acknowledged boss of the valley, but things are different now. We haven't enough men to fight it out with Dyson but, if the law moved in, then folk in River Bend would come over openly to our side. We'd get rid of the rustlers for good. Don't you agree?'

Marsh said carefully: 'I reckon there's something in what you say, Grace, but remember, your father's a sick man — he isn't prepared to admit he needs the law's help. Best humour him, I guess.'

The girl watched Marsh's face.

'You know the reason, don't you, Pete? Can't you tell me?'

Marsh shifted his feet awkwardly.

'I reckon your father has good reason for what he does — and you don't have to worry about Dyson. I'll look after him for yuh. River Bend will soon swing over to our side when they see what's happening.'

'I wonder.' Grace Hammond looked unhappy. 'You're going into town alone? Is that wise?'

Marsh drawled: 'I'll be all right.'

She said: 'And afterward, Pete, what then? You can't remain on the run all your life. You've got to square yourself with the law some time.'

Marsh didn't like to think about that. He wanted to marry Grace and offer her a home — but could he expect her to throw in her lot with a wanted man? He sighed. His life was a mess and he couldn't see the end of the trail.

He said: 'It'll work out, Grace.'

He turned to mount his horse, but Grace caught his arm.

'Pete, oh Pete, I love you. I couldn't bear it if anything happened to you. Come back to me, Pete — we'll make a future together somehow . . .'

Marsh was surprised by her desperate eagerness, overwhelmed by the force of her love. He found himself trembling as she clung to him. He kissed her.

'I'll come back, Grace,' he said softly. 'And I'll come to yuh a free man — I promise that.'

'I'll wait, Pete. I'll wait for you till we can be together, always.'

He pushed her away from him and

climbed into the saddle. She waved as he rode off, but he did not look back.

Marsh set Starlight at a gallop and the sable gelding with white markings responded eagerly, glad of the exercise after two days in the stables. The trail to River Bend was flat and empty of life; Marsh passed clusters of pine, covered miles of bare grassland, taking little notice of the view. He thought of Grace, of her love for him, and of his future. Somehow, he had to clear himself with the law for her sake — but how? How?

It was a problem he could not solve. He considered giving himself up, and imagined the years in prison. Years without sight of the woman he loved. Could she wait that long?

He was coming up to the bluff where Stoat had ambushed him. Marsh pushed thoughts of Grace Hammond from his mind and swung off the trail. It was unlikely that Dyson would try the same game twice, but he'd be ready if anyone waited for him. He rode in close to the bluff, watching the trees that grew on the ochre-coloured slopes.

There was a break in the wall of the bluff, and a gully leading farther away from the trail. A horseman waited there. Marsh recognised him — Fingle! Marsh's hand flew to his gun; he drew, and fired a warning shot. He'd told Fingle to leave the valley, yet the ex-foreman was still here. Marsh went after him, intent on keeping his promise.

Fingle did not wait to fire back. He turned his horse and rode deeper into the gully. Marsh plunged in after him, shouting.

'I'm coming for yuh, Fingle — stand and shoot it out, you yellow rat!'

Fingle did not stop. He turned his head, looked back, then he rode on at break-neck speed. Marsh followed, riding between the narrowing walls of the gully. It flashed into his mind that this could be a trap, but he never hesitated in the chase. Fingle had told Grace he was an outlaw — and that was something Marsh could never forgive.

If it was a trap, Marsh would shoot his way out and the ambushers would regret their recklessness in trying to trick him. It was Fingle that Marsh wanted. He galloped deeper into the gully, his gun ready for a shot.

Round a bend in the high walls, Fingle had stopped. It was a dead end. Fingle had turned to face him, a rifle across the mane of his horse. Marsh knew then that he had ridden into a trap; Fingle would never have stood alone against him. He started to check Starlight's pace, his eyes going to the rock walls, searching for the men who would be there. He spotted them too late —

A lariat snaked down from above, the noose settling skilfully about Marsh's broad shoulders. The rope jerked tight, imprisoning his arms and dragging him clear of the saddle. He hit the ground with a force that drove the wind from his lungs; his Colt went flying from his grasp.

A bulky figure jumped down, slammed a gun barrel across his skull. As he blacked out, he had a vague image of a slim man winding in the lariat . . .

Pete Marsh was not unconscious many minutes. He came to, his head aching and rawhide cutting into the flesh of his arms. After a moment, his eyes opened to focus on the effeminate figure of Claude Dyson. Dyson took snuff, and drawled:

'You're not so smart after all, Marsh. I would never have ridden into a trap as you did. Fingle was only the bait — as you know now.'

Marsh said nothing. Dyson was not alone; the bald-headed Stoat was with him and the slim man in thigh-high boots. Fingle was grinning in a way that would have chilled a lesser man's blood. Four to one. Marsh thought calmly, and my arms are tied. This looks like the end . . .

'Let me do it,' Fingle said. 'You saw the way he beat me up — let me finish him, Dyson.'

Dyson frowned.

'I'm the boss here, Fingle. I'll decide what happens to Marsh — not you.'

Fingle had lapsed into sulky silence. Marsh looked round him; his horse had been staked down and his guns removed. Both Stoat and the slim man held Colts in their hands. There was little hope of a break for freedom.

Dyson studied him, thoughtfully.

'You know, Marsh,' he said smoothly. 'I'm still inclined to give yuh a chance. You're a wanted man — and fighting on the wrong side. I'd like to have you with me — '

Marsh snapped: 'You're wasting yore time! I'm going to run you crooks out of the valley.'

Fingle broke in: 'You see, Dyson, he won't change sides. I told yuh that — now let me have him!'

Stoat growled: 'Shut up, Fingle. You're small fry around here.'

Marsh faced Dyson coolly. The leader of the outlaws looked a dandy in his crimson jacket and bottle-green trousers. He was handsome, too, with dark, curly hair. It was his eyes that revealed his true character, cold and snakelike, cunning eyes filled with treachery. Marsh knew he could expect no mercy from Claude Dyson.

Dyson said: 'If we kill Marsh, we'll set the whole valley against us. He's popular in River Bend, too popular. We won't kill him, not till he's discredited before everyone's eyes. We've got to show him running from us . . . then the town will go to sleep and we can run things as before.' He smiled, a cruel smile with no pity in it. 'We won't kill him. Instead, we'll turn him loose and send him to River Bend!'

Fingle stared at Dyson in disbelief.

'You're crazy,' he said. 'You must kill him! You must — '

Stoat pushed his hand into Fingle's face, and shoved.

'Shut up,' he snarled. 'The boss decides things here!'

Marsh waited, wondering what Dyson had in mind for him, and knowing it would not be pleasant. He kept a poker face, stood completely still, hoping for a chance to turn the tables on his captors.

Dyson said: 'Slim, fetch me two large rocks.'

Slim holstered his gun and walked off. He dragged one chunk of rock back to Marsh's side and went after another. The second rock was slightly smaller, with a sharp jag projecting from it.

Stoat was curious. He asked:

'What yuh gonna do, boss?'

Dyson smiled evilly.

'What is it that makes Marsh dangerous? Only one thing — the fact of his being a fast gun-slinger. Well, we're going to change that. I'm going to smash Marsh's gun-hand!' He laughed, pleased with his own subtlety. 'Do you think he'll stand against us when we ride into River Bend, and he can't pull a gun? Or will he run? I think he'll run . . . and the townsfolk will see who's boss in Gunsmoke Valley!'

Marsh caught his breath. For a gunman to lose the use of his gun-hand spelt finish! Dyson's plan was clever, devilish. He struggled to break free — and Stoat used his gun-butt again, driving him to the ground.

Marsh lay still, dazed. His right arm was freed and held in place on top of one rock. He hadn't the strength to fight off the men who held him. His right hand lay exposed . . .

'You're a clever man, Dyson,' Fingle said admiringly. 'I'd never have thought of that. Marsh will be helpless — why, I'll be able to pull a gun on him myself!'

Stoat was sarcastic.

'Yeah,' the bald man said. 'I reckon you're a real hero, all right!'

Dyson stooped and lifted the second chunk of rock; he stood over Marsh, legs apart, balanced, juggling the rock in his hands till the sharp jag pointed downwards. He smiled brutally.

'Hold him still.'

Stoat and Slim put pressure on the half-conscious Marsh.

'Now,' said Dyson, and brought down the rock with all his strength.

Marsh caught his breath, trying to break free. He could not move. His right arm was helpless. The rock crashed down on his hand, splintering the bone. Sharp agony shot up his arm; tears came to his eyes and sweat poured off his face. He bit his lip and tasted blood, but he did not cry out.

Dyson dropped the rock at his feet, laughing.

'That settles you, Marsh — your gun-fighting days are over. Now try to stop us entering River Bend!'

Marsh swore in a low, painful voice, sobbing. 'I'll get you for sure . . . '

His words tailed off and he lay on the ground, panting, the throbbing in his hand so great that he nearly fainted. He nursed his hand to his chest, feeling the broken bone. He rocked to and fro, the blood staining his shirt. There was a dark mist settling over his eyes.

Dyson said: 'Rope him to his horse.'

Slim stripped the saddle from Starlight and Stoat threw Marsh across the gelding's back. Fingle roped him down.

The four outlaws mounted their horses and Dyson took Starlight's reins, leading the way out of the gully. On the trail to River Bend, Claude Dyson turned Starlight loose, pointing the gelding's head towards town. Savagely, he brought down his quirt on Starlight's rump, and the horse, whinnying shrilly, bolted.

Marsh lifted his head, staring back in blind rage. There was a terrible light in his grey eyes as he watched the four outlaws ride off. The pain in his hand annoyed him. Tied down in an uncomfortable position, he could do nothing to control his mount. Starlight galloped madly, stung by the quirt and not understanding what had happened to his master. He raced on, and Marsh was shaken by every jolt of the wild ride.

He began to black out. His head was pointing at the ground, the blood rushed to his temples. He saw only the bare earth and brown grass of the prairie, knew only the greatest agony.

He felt himself slipping into a dark oblivion . . .

Starlight slowed after a time, but still went on for the distant town. The gelding carried Pete Marsh into River Bend, into Main Street, where a crowd quickly gathered to see what had happened. They lifted the unconscious Marsh from his horse and carried him to Doc Turner's . . . a gunman with his gun-hand broken!

9

Left-Handed Vengeance!

Grace Hammond heard the news about Marsh when she drove the hay-wagon into town next day. She made straight for Doc Turner's house, but never arrived there. Turner came down the street, smoking a cheroot.

Grace said quickly: 'How's Pete? I only just heard — why didn't someone ride out and tell me yesterday?'

Turner raised his black, flat-crowned hat to her.

'Marsh is more stubborn than a corral-full of mules! He's the worst patient I ever had. In comparison with him, your father is a lamb. He ought to be in bed, resting — instead of which, he's up and active. Hear that?'

Grace listened. The distant sound of gunshots came to her.

Turner said: 'He's on the waste lot, the other end of town. He's borrowed a Colt and bought a box of ammunition and, right now, he's practising shooting with his left hand. I guess he's a man who only knows one thing . . . fighting back. No one came out to the ranch because Marsh forbade it; he didn't want yuh worried.'

The girl smiled faintly.

'That sounds like Pete. It's true then, his hand is smashed?'

Doc Turner nodded.

'True enough. The bone in his right hand is broken — it'll be months before he can use it. Even then, he'll never draw a gun again, with any speed. So he's learning to shoot left-handed.'

Grace said nothing. She left the doctor and hurried down Main Street, anxious to see Marsh. Beyond the saloons and stores and the double row of wooden shacks, a patch of waste ground used for dumping rubbish extended outwards from the rim of the town towards the prairie. Pete Marsh stood in the centre of the waste lot, a half-used box of cartridges on the ground beside him; he fired at a target chalked on the trunk of a cottonwood — and the holes in the target told more plainly than words that he was as deadly with his left hand as with his right.

Marsh was so intent on his practice that he did not see the girl approach. Grace waited a little way off, watching him. His right hand was in wooden splints, bandaged, his arm in a sling about his neck and held against his chest. He used a heavy Colt .45, drawing and firing, returning the gun to his waist holster. She observed that he had changed the position of his holster, for ease of drawing. When he exhausted the gun's chambers, he tucked the Colt's muzzle under his injured right arm, grabbed shells from the box with his left hand, and reloaded.

Then he commenced shooting all over again. Grace watched him through the whole operation several times before she spoke.

'Is your hand hurting you, Pete?'

He lowered his gun and turned. The determination that made his eyes appear cast in grey metal softened as he saw her.

'Some,' he admitted. 'I can stand it.'

He emptied his gun and started to reload again.

Grace Hammond said: 'It doesn't look to me as if you need so much practice. You're hitting the target every time.'

'My left hand's accurate enough,' Marsh replied, 'but I've no speed. I'm too slow on the draw, and loading — and that could be fatal.'

'Well,' Grace said, 'you'd best come back to the ranch. You can't stay here and fight Dyson's outfit with one hand.'

Pete Marsh fired steadily at the chalked target till his gun was empty. He tucked his Colt under his right arm, picked up fresh shells and started pushing them into the empty chambers. Grace saw that he had difficulty with the operation.

'I'll load for you, Pete — '

He pushed her roughly away from him.

'No, Grace. I have to learn to do this myself.'

She flared up, angry with him: 'Don't be so obstinate, Pete! I only want to help you.'

He holstered his Colt and stood looking at her, unsmiling.

'Go back to the ranch and stay there. Dyson smashed my hand because he reckons I'll run when he comes into town. He never made a bigger mistake. I'm staying till he rides in. I'm staying to shoot it out with him.'

Grace asked: 'With your left hand?'

'Yes.'

'Then you're a stubborn fool, Pete Marsh.'

'Maybe,' Marsh drawled easily. 'But I'm not running before Dyson and his carrion.'

Grace sighed. He was beyond argument, she saw. There was something in his eyes that frightened her — a tenacious fury that came near to madness. He had made up his mind to beat Dyson one-handed, and he would — or go down fighting. She admired his spirit — and hated his stubbornness.

Marsh faced his target again, fell into a crouch and drew his Colt; he triggered, and red flame spurted from the muzzle, spouting lead. The air was noisy with gunshots, acrid with the taste of cordite.

Grace said: 'I shall stay in town, and send word for our riders to come out. This isn't your private fight, Pete — and you can't face Dyson alone.'

She wheeled about and walked quickly down Main Street. Marsh watched her go, shrugged, and continued his practice. He used up the box of shells and, satisfied with his progress left the waste lot. He turned into a bar and called for a drink.

No one spoke to him. Men moved casually out of his way. All River Bend left him alone; Dyson would be coming soon and no one reckoned that Marsh had a chance. Marsh's lips curled in disgust as he stared round the saloon. These were the men who had shouted for a leader — now they stood aside, afraid to come over on what they considered to be the losing side. Dyson had been clever in smashing his gun-hand . . .

Marsh clumsily rolled a cigarette with his left hand and lit up. The taste of the tobacco soothed his nerves. His injured hand still pained him and he had to be careful not to knock it. He walked along the boardwalk, to let everyone see he was staying for the showdown.

Faces watched from windows. The street was almost deserted. He moved past the false-front of River Bend's only hotel, past the saloons and stores, the freighting office and a line of wooden shacks. Outside the Pine Roost stables,

Doc Turner and Joe Brett were sitting on a bench, and each man had a rifle across his knees.

Marsh walked over to them.

'Thanks for bringing in my saddle, Joe,' he said.

The odd-job man nodded.

'That's all right, Pete. Glad to do any little thing for yuh. Starlight's saddled and ready when you want him.'

Turner squinted at the trail leading into town, and shifted his rifle.

'Seeing that you're set on staying,' he drawled, 'Joe and me figured yuh might need a little help. We'll be around when the trouble starts.'

Marsh smiled gravely. It warmed him to know that he had two men he could rely on, but it wasn't their fight.

He said: 'Thanks, but this is my show. You keep out of it. You can do one thing for me though — tell me when Dyson hits town. And then keep an eye on Grace Hammond for me, because I don't want her taking a hand in the fighting.'

'I'll watch out for her,' Turner promised.

Marsh walked back up Main Street, taking his time. He wished Dyson would show up and get it over. He dropped in at another saloon and took a second drink before continuing his promenade.

There was an air of tension in River Bend. Few folk showed themselves and some of the stores had closed; wooden shutters had been placed over the glass windows. Further up, Marsh saw Grace supervising the loading of the Hammond wagon.

'It's just about ready to go,' she told him. 'I'm paying a man to drive it back for me. I'm staying to look after you.'

She carried a rifle in her hand and her face had that stubborn set that told Marsh it was useless arguing with her.

'Keep off the street,' he said briefly.

Grace nodded.

'I'll be at a window. Pete, be careful — for my sake.'

'I'll be careful,' Marsh said, and walked on.

He saw the hay wagon leave town and Grace go into the hotel. A few minutes later, a second-storey window opened and he saw the curtain drawn back. He turned and went south again.

It was daylight, but there was little sun. A cold wind swept the open street, driving a cloud of dust before it. A few snowflakes fell. Someone had got drunk and was singing raucously in a nearby saloon. Marsh moved through the swing-doors and up to the counter.

'Say, fellar,' slurred the drunk, peering at Marsh. 'Have a drink with me. Barman, pour this fellar some whisky.'

The barman poured another drink and pushed it along the counter. Marsh took it, and said: 'Thanks.'

The drunk propped himself against the bar. He was a lean man with stubble on his chin and a large stetson that kept flopping down over his eyes. He pushed it back repeatedly.

164

'Going to be a killing,' he mumbled. 'Fellar named Marsh. Better keep off the streets, 'less yuh want to collect some lead.'

The barman said, sharply: 'Shut up. This is Marsh!' He looked uneasily at Pete Marsh. 'Al means no harm — it's just that he's taken too much liquor aboard.'

'He don't worry me any,' Marsh drawled. 'Let him talk. It makes a change to have someone in this town talk to me.'

The barman moved to the other end of the counter. Al, who had started singing again, suddenly stopped. He pushed his hat back from his eyes and stared suspiciously at Marsh.

'You're Marsh?' he said in wonder. 'Why don't yuh get on yore horse and get out of town?'

'I like it here,' Marsh said, sipping his whisky slowly. 'I'll like it better when Dyson shows up. I want to see his face just before I kill him!'

Al shuddered.

'I don't like all this talk of killing. It was quiet before you come to the valley.'

Marsh said: 'It'll always be quiet when folk are too scared to stand up and fight crooks like Dyson. It's quiet on Boot Hill, too.'

Al left the counter and swayed drunkenly. He poked a finger at Marsh's sling.

'How yuh going to draw a gun in that thing?'

'I've another hand,' Pete Marsh said, and drew his Colt left-handed.

Al shook his head.

'Fast, but not fast enough. Dyson'll kill yuh for sure!'

The barman came back in a hurry.

'Shut up! Shut up, Al!' he hissed.

Marsh said: 'Let him be,' and dropped the Colt in its holster.

Al went back to singing again, his hat over his eyes. He had a loud, unmusical voice and seemed determined to tell all River Bend how he had once loved a Mexican girl. Marsh finished his drink, made another quirley and sat smoking. There was coldness in him, but no fear. He waited for Dyson to come, hated the waiting and wished the fight would start. Maybe he wouldn't live through it, but he wouldn't run — and some of Dyson's men would die before he did.

Al got tired of singing and called for another drink. Marsh bought him one, but took nothing himself. Al wanted to start a fight over that.

'You think I ain't good enough to drink with yuh,' he accused. 'Waal, let me tell you — '

'Shut up, Al,' the barman said furiously.

Marsh lost interest in them as the batwings swung open and Doc Turner entered the saloon. Turner had an unlit cheroot clamped between his teeth and a rifle in his hands.

He said: 'Pete, Stoat's just ridden into town, alone. Joe's watching the trail for the others.'

Marsh rose to his feet, stubbing out

his cigarette. He hitched up his gun-belt.

'Thanks, Doc,' he said. 'Now keep off the street. This is between me and Stoat.'

He walked to the door and went out. Turner called after him: 'Good luck, Pete!'

Marsh paused on the boardwalk outside the saloon, staring the length of Main Street. Farther down, a bulky man hitched his horse to a rail. There was no one else in sight. Where were Dyson and the others? Marsh was suspicious, trying to figure out what their absence meant. Maybe Dyson was so sure he'd run that he hadn't bothered to send more than one man. Well, that suited Marsh — and Dyson would get a shock.

He moved deliberately from the boardwalk, going down the steps and reaching the centre of the dirt street. He walked slowly forward, quite calm, ignoring the ache in his shattered hand. The fingers of his left hand crushed the butt of his low-slung .45.

Stoat turned from hitching his horse. He saw Marsh and came eagerly towards him, anticipating an easy victory. His bald head and scarred face gave him a venomous appearance, and his eyes, close-set about an eagle's beak nose, held the desire to kill. He licked his lips, noting that Marsh's right arm was in a sling, his only gun on the left side.

'You, Marsh,' he called. 'You've been told to clear out of town. You going — or d'yuh want to shoot it out?'

Marsh said nothing, advancing steadily. He guessed that Dyson had told the bald man to try and force him to run — that way, all resistance to the rustlers in River Bend would end.

Stoat shouted again: 'All right, if yuh want to die, stand and draw!'

Marsh closed the gap, watching Stoat's hands closely. The bald man had dropped into a killer's crouch. Marsh stopped, fifteen paces off. His body was taut, his mind clear and calm. He had to remember he wasn't fast with his left hand. He had to make the first shot count.

Stoat snarled: 'Now!' and went for his guns.

Marsh side-stepped, drawing his Colt and bringing it up, his arm straight and level with his shoulder. Stoat's guns crashed flame and lead but Marsh's side movement saved him. One slug tore past his head, another chewed the flesh from his side. He aimed carefully and squeezed the trigger. The Colt jumped in his hand as crimson flame streaked from the muzzle. His shot went true — Stoat staggered in his stride, stumbled forward.

Marsh let his gun-arm fall to his side, blue smoke curling up from the muzzle. Stoat lay unmoving on the ground, arms under him, face in the dust and his bulky body doubled up. Marsh walked up and turned the bald man over with his foot. He was dead; the shot had gone clean into his heart.

Marsh looked beyond the dead man,

watching the street for any sign of Dyson. There was no one. He holstered his gun, relaxing, suddenly conscious of a smarting pain in his side.

Doc Turner and Grace came running from cover. Joe Brett appeared on the street.

'No sign of the rest of Dyson's outfit,' Brett reported. 'Can't understand Stoat coming alone, but there it is.'

'You're hurt, Pete,' Grace said. 'Doc, do something.'

Marsh went into Turner's house and pulled off his shirt. There was blood on his vest and a nasty gash where Stoat's shell had ripped through him.

Doc bathed and dressed the wound.

'Nothing to worry about,' he said. 'It missed the rib bone and will heal in a couple of days. Just take things easy for a spell.'

Grace Hammond laughed wryly.

'What a hope, Doc! He gets beaten up, shot in the head, and has his hand smashed — yet he still insists on meeting Dyson alone. Now he's killed

Dyson's right-hand man, and that means trouble will be coming fast. Take it easy, you say!'

'I'm still alive,' Marsh protested mildly.

Grace snapped: 'But for how long? By the time you get around to marrying me, there won't be much left for me to take care of. You'll get yourself shot to pieces!'

Marsh made himself comfortable in a chair and lit a cigarette. He was feeling limp after the moment of tension. He grinned at the girl.

'Stop worrying about me. I can take care of myself and I sure aim to come out of this alive. I've good reason — you!'

Turner went to the door as rapid hoofbeats sounded.

'Someone coming to town at a helluva lick.' He opened the door to see a rider dismount in a flurry of dust. 'It's Carey,' he said.

Grace Hammond moved quickly to the door, followed by Marsh. Carey crossed the street to them, and Marsh knew by the man's face that he had bad news.

'Miss Hammond,' Carey blurted out, 'yore father's dead. Murdered! He was shot down in cold blood, by Claude Dyson!'

Grace said, 'Oh!' and went white. Marsh caught her arm to steady her. He cursed in a low, bitter voice. He knew now why Stoat had been alone . . .

10

The Law's Deputy

'I take it there's been gunplay at the Hammond ranch,' Doc Turner said in a brisk, practical tone. 'Does anyone there need my professional aid?'

Carey shook his head.

'It's too late for that, Doc. The cook was the only other person on the ranch when Dyson struck. He got shot, too. He was breathing his last when I left . . . '

Marsh threw his cigarette to the ground and stamped it in the dust. He was trembling with fury. That gunmen should seek out and ruthlessly murder an old man was something he could not forgive; he swore to avenge Roger Hammond's death. Dyson would pay with his own life.

He took Grace gently by the arm and

led her inside the shack, sitting her down. Turner poured her a glass of brandy.

'Drink this, Miss Hammond,' he said. 'You've had a shock — you'd better rest here a-while. Carey, help yourself to whisky.'

Grace Hammond sipped at the brandy and, slowly, the colour returned to her cheeks. She sat quite still, rigid, saying nothing. Carey tossed back a tumbler of whisky and looked straight at Marsh.

'I'll get the boys together,' he said briefly. 'It's time to clean out those killers on south side.'

Turner interrupted: 'Hold yore hosses! Let's get the story straight, first. What exactly happened at the ranch? You sure it was Dyson?'

Carey pushed back a lock of lank grey hair, his blue eyes as cold as ice.

'It was like this,' he began. 'I was with the rest of the boys, tending the cattle in the basin. We needed more feeding stuff, so I went back to the ranch to see if Miss Hammond had returned. It was quiet when I rode into the patio — then I saw Mr Hammond. He was lying on the veranda, dead. I reckon he had about a dozen slugs in him — '

Grace shuddered.

'All right,' Turner said quickly. 'Just give us the facts.'

Carey went on: 'There wasn't anything I could do for him, so I looked for Cookie. He was on the ground, with a gun still in his hand. He'd been shot in the stomach and left to die. He was still conscious, but all I could do was to give him a little water. I knew he'd be dead before I could get help. He managed to tell me what happened.'

'Dyson rode in with Slim and Fingle. They caught Mr Hammond by surprise — didn't give him a chance — just shot him to pieces. Cookie tried to stop them leaving, but he only got shot for his trouble. They rode off, laughing.'

Marsh swore.

'I'll get them,' he said. 'I'm riding straight out to Dyson's place. Carey, you get the boys together and follow as fast as yuh can. We'll settle this now.'

He moved for the door, hitching his gun-belt, but stopped as Grace rose and said:

'No, Pete. I don't want it to be like that. Revenge only breeds more trouble. I want my father's murderers brought in for trial. I want the law in Gunsmoke Valley. We'll wait till the sheriff arrives; we can form a posse and do what has to be done legally.'

Doc Turner added: 'I agree with Miss Hammond. We need the sheriff here. I'm all for cleaning out that snakes' nest, but we must have the law on our side.'

Carey said nothing. He looked at Marsh, waiting.

'If that's how you want it, Grace,' Pete Marsh said slowly, 'that's how it'll be. It's for you to say. But first, I must speak with you alone. There's something you don't know, that you ought to know now.'

Carey walked out without a word.

Turner paused in the doorway.

'Grace,' he said, 'don't take this hard. Yore dad was a sick man; he hadn't long to live.'

He closed the door behind him, leaving Marsh alone with the girl.

'Well, Pete,' she said calmly. 'What is it?'

Marsh took a deep breath. He didn't quite know how to begin, but he knew this had to be said.

'I'm going to tell yuh why yore father didn't want the law in Gunsmoke Valley. He didn't want you to know, but I reckon the position has changed; anyway, you can decide whether or not I'm doing the right thing. It's like this — '

Grace Hammond did not speak. She sat down again, waiting, her eyes on Marsh's face.

'Yore father set out to build a cattle empire, and he succeeded; but he wasn't always particular about his methods. He used force when smaller men stood against him. He went outside the law and hired gunmen and cattle-thieves to carry out his orders without question. He took over the valley with guns. You can see now why he didn't want the law here — he daren't allow it. Dyson was working for him, remember, till they quarrelled; it was he who ran the gunmen for Roger Hammond.'

Grace nodded. Marsh's news did not seem to upset her as much as he had expected.

'It always puzzled me why Dad kept him around. Now I understand. I'm glad you told me, Pete — thank you.'

Marsh said: 'You've got to understand, Grace, that if you bring in the sheriff you may lose yore claim to the range-land. The law likely won't hold your father's claim as legal on account of his methods.'

'I understand that,' the girl said. 'Dad did wrong, but there's nothing anyone can do to change that now. I shall still bring in the sheriff, even if I lose everything.'

'You're sure, Grace?'

'Quite sure!'

Marsh laid his hand on her shoulder and squeezed.

'I reckon yore Dad would be proud of yuh, Grace. He knew he was wrong, and that's why he wanted me to fight Dyson — to make the valley safe for you. We'll see it through together.'

She looked up at him.

'But you, Pete? You're wanted by the law.'

Marsh smiled.

'Don't start worrying about me; I can look after myself.'

Grace Hammond sighed.

'That's just what I don't want — you fighting the law, always on the run, a price on your head. You can't go on like that for the rest of your life.'

'I don't intend to,' Marsh replied. 'I'll bring the sheriff here myself.'

Grace rose to her feet, smiling sadly.

'Pete, tell me the truth. Was it because of me that you turned outlaw? Because I laughed at you and said I

180

wouldn't marry a cowhand?'

Marsh did not answer. He looked down at the floor because he could not look into her eyes and speak a lie.

Grace said: 'So it was, Pete! I've a lot to make up to you. It seems I'm no better than my father.'

Marsh shook his head at her.

'That's no way to talk, Grace. You and your father are no worse than a hundred other men setting up a home in the West. This is a rough country, and only big men with hard ways can start from nothing and build for the future. Someone always gets hurt in the rush to open up a new land — but it's changing. The old days have gone for good. The law will move in and straighten things out but without yore father, and men like him, none of this would be possible.'

He paused, and Grace said:

'I suppose you're right. You're quite a philosopher, Pete, but we have to be practical. There's still Dyson to deal with.'

181

Marsh held her a moment, and kissed her.

'I'm going for the sheriff now. You sit tight till I come back, and don't worry. Everything will work out in the end.'

He left her, opened the door and walked across the street to the Pine Roost stables. Joe Brett had Starlight ready for him.

'Reckoned you'd be riding directly,' the odd-job man drawled. 'You got some backing in town since yuh downed Stoat.'

Marsh climbed into the saddle.

'Tell Doc Turner to hold them,' he called. 'I'm going for the sheriff. We're going to do this the lawful way.'

He rode off, out of River Bend, to the west. Blue Forks, where the county sheriff had his office, was forty-odd miles away. Marsh set the gelding at a canter and took the journey steadily. The miles flew by, miles of open rangeland once he was clear of the valley; he followed the course of the

182

river as it tumbled down the slopes of high tableland. Further on, the pines thinned out and grass gave way to cacti. He struck across scrubland and bare desert, heading for the town nestling in the distant hills.

Marsh had given up thinking about the future. Grace might well lose the ranch — he might go to gaol. There didn't seem any way of dealing with the situation. The law must come to Gunsmoke Valley, and the law must take its course. Pete Marsh rode with a blank mind and a set purpose.

It was late afternoon when he rode down the trail between the hills, into Blue Forks. The town was growing, straggling out in crooked lines of wooden shacks from the main cross-roads. Starlight walked the main thoroughfare, between saloons and stores and corrals. Beyond the stagepost and the dance hall, next to the sprawling façade of the Grande Hotel, the law office and gaol squatted; a square building of adobe brick and bleached grey paintwork.

Marsh came out of his saddle and hitched Starlight to the rail. He went up the steps. The door of the law office was open and the notice proclaimed:

H. Brownsides — Sheriff.

Marsh went through the open door, cradling his injured arm against his chest. He kept a poker face, but his pulse was jumping. So much depended on the sort of man Brownsides was.

It was a small office with a desk and one spare chair. A narrow passage led back to the cells and a raw-boned man in black suiting sat behind the desk; his coat was open, showing a silver star pinned to his shirt. Marsh studied the sheriff and was impressed. Brownsides looked about forty, a veteran of the West; he had a long, clean-shaven jaw and drooping moustache. He wore a single revolver in a waist holster. His stone-grey eyes settled on Marsh.

'Waal, stranger, what can I do to help you?' the sheriff drawled.

'I'm Pete Marsh.'

Brownsides did not stir in his chair.

184

His eyes revealed a spark of interest, no more. He said:

'Take a seat, Marsh,' and fumbled in a drawer of his desk, pulling out a sheaf of Wanted notices. He leafed through them, ignoring Marsh till he found the one he wanted. He looked up, unsmiling.

'You got anything to say before I throw yuh in gaol?' he asked bluntly.

Marsh rolled and lit a cigarette, left-handed. He blew a stream of smoke across the office, leaned forward in his chair, and said:

'Roger Hammond's dead. Dyson murdered him. You're needed in Gunsmoke Valley.'

Brownsides let out his breath in a hiss.

'So! It's come at last. Can't say I haven't been expecting something like this. How is Miss Hammond taking it?'

Marsh said: 'It was she who sent me for you.'

'And where do you fit into all this?' Brownsides asked politely.

'I came back to ask Grace Hammond to marry me. Roger Hammond asked me to help him fight Dyson.'

'And Miss Hammond sent yuh for me? Sensible girl that — got more savvy than her father.' The sheriff studied the Wanted notice he still held in his hand. 'She agreed to marry yuh?'

'Yes,' said Pete Marsh calmly. 'She's going to wait for me.'

Brownsides didn't speak for some minutes. He appeared lost in thought. Marsh said:

'You going to Gunsmoke Valley, sheriff?'

Brownsides nodded, and pulled on one side of his moustache.

'I'll be going, Marsh, in good time. The law doesn't hurry, but it's sure. I'll hang Dyson in due course. You now, you look as if yuh been in trouble. Gun-hand broken?'

Marsh held out his right hand, bandaged and in splints.

'I fell into Dyson's trap. He smashed it between two rocks, thinking I'd run. I shot his lieutenant with my left hand.'

'Hmm,' said the sheriff.

There was another pause, then Brownsides asked:

'You're still young, Marsh. Still want to play badman? Or yuh wanting to settle down and start afresh?'

'I want to marry Grace — and I want to go to her with a clean record.'

Sheriff Brownsides rose to his feet; he crumpled up Marsh's Wanted notice and tossed it in the waste basket.

'You're not wanted in Arizona, and I've never seen this,' he drawled. 'I've a heap of respect for Miss Hammond's judgment, and if she's got faith in yuh, that's good enough for me. Listen: I've kept out of Gunsmoke Valley because Hammond was running things peaceably. I heard about the trouble starting, and I heard about you coming back to the valley — so I waited to see what would happen. Now I'm ready to move in for the clean-up.

'You've been fighting on the right side since yuh returned, and I reckon that squares anything you may have done in the past. I don't believe in holding grudges. You're young enough to make a fresh start, and I'm going to give you the chance. The West needs good men, and I'd sooner save a man than hang him. Marsh, I'm going to make you my deputy and that will square yuh with the law!'

Pete Marsh felt he must be dreaming.

'Stand up,' Brownsides said. 'Hold this.' He handed him a bible. 'I'm swearing you in as a deputy. Repeat after me — '

Marsh spoke the oath and the sheriff pinned a silver star to his chest.

'If yuh go back on that oath,' Brownsides said quietly, 'I'll hunt you down and kill yuh with my own hands. Don't ever forget that.'

Marsh took a long breath.

'Sheriff,' he replied, 'you won't regret this. Thanks. You've made a new man of me — you and Grace Hammond.'

'All right, Marsh. Now go and get some food while I put my things together. Then we'll be riding.'

Marsh paused, uncertain.

'There's one other thing, sheriff. Miss Hammond. Will she keep the range now her father's dead? I guess it's no secret how he obtained his power.'

Brownsides shrugged.

'I guess she's little to worry about. Westerners aren't the sort to take revenge on a woman. Maybe some adjustments will need to be made, but I reckon she'll come out of it all right. The past is past. No good digging up old grudges — and who's to say who the land rightfully belongs to?'

Marsh walked to a restaurant down the street with an easy mind. His problems seemed to be resolving themselves for him — there was only Dyson to deal with, then he would be free to marry Grace. He ate a large meal of beefsteak and vegetables with relish, finding himself acutely hungry. He had just finished his coffee and smoked a cigarette when Brownsides called for him.

The sheriff had a slicker over his clothes and his horse waited outside.

'All set, Marsh? Let's ride!'

Pete Marsh mounted Starlight and cantered out of Blue Forks alongside the sheriff. They took the trail for River Bend, riding at a fast trot, neither man speaking. Marsh felt as if a great weight had been lifted from his shoulders. He was free, free to start a new life, to marry and make a home.

The wind had straightened, driving icily across the open plain. Snowflakes came faster. Heavy clouds pressed lower, darkening the sky. Night was not far off.

Brownsides said: 'I don't like this. Reckon there's a blizzard blowing up — the wrong weather for our job.'

They kept on, entering Gunsmoke Valley and using the trail by the river. The waters swirled blackly, and the snow fell faster. It was quite dark when they saw the lights of River Bend ahead.

Marsh and the sheriff quickened their pace for the town, riding down the slope into a blaze of yellow oil-light. There was noise and movement on the streets, and it seemed as if a great crowd had gathered.

'Something's happened,' Marsh snapped, and went forward at the gallop.

He saw riders preparing to leave town; grim-faced men with guns and ropes. He recognised Carey and Lefty and Smith with other 'punchers from the Hammond ranch. He saw Joe Brett and Doc Turner and tradesmen from the town. It looked like an unofficial posse was setting out. Carey saw Marsh, and shouted:

'Dyson burnt down the Hammond place — and Fingle has Grace a prisoner!'

11

Trapped

Grace Hammond watched Marsh leave River Bend, and felt suddenly alone and frightened. Her father was dead. The man she loved had ridden off to face the law. Dyson was still free and, until his power in Gunsmoke Valley was broken, she could not live without fear. Meanwhile, the ranch and cattle — her ranch and her cattle now — lay unprotected.

She must pull herself together. She had her father's blood in her veins, and he had been a fighter; he had never shirked his responsibility, no matter how he felt personally. She must return to the ranch at once.

Carey waited for her on the street.

'I'll be riding back to fetch the boys,' he said. 'You'll wait here for the sheriff,

Miss Hammond.'

'No, Carey,' the girl said calmly. 'I'm coming back with you. I must see that my father's body is cared for. Besides, the ranch and cattle must be guarded. Dyson doesn't know yet that Pete shot Stoat; he'll be thinking he has a free hand to do as he likes. He may attack again.'

Grace had driven into town on the wagon. Now, she needed a horse. Stoat's brown mare was still hitched to the rail, and he wouldn't be needing her again; she untied the horse and swung herself into the saddle.

Doc Turner came up as they were about to leave.

'Doc,' she said, 'you've some authority in town. Use it to see someone doesn't start a lynching party. Make them wait for the sheriff to arrive. We want the law behind us when we go after Dyson.'

Turner nodded.

'I'll do that, Miss Hammond, I'll send someone out to the ranch when the sheriff gets here.'

Grace and Carey left town, crossed the river and headed back for the ranch. They spoke hardly at all. Carey was thinking of the fight to come and kept a sharp watch for Dyson's riders. Grace thought of her father, and braced herself for the moment when she must see him.

She sat stiffly in the saddle, a girl of twenty-two, lovely to look at with her sun-tanned complexion and rich dark hair. She had the bearing of an older woman, the calmness and self-confidence of maturity. If she had been spoilt and wayward when Marsh had left the valley, she was changed now. She had grown up and was ready to take her place in the West.

Coming into the patio, Carey said:

'You wait off a little, Miss Hammond, while I set things straight. They ain't nice to look at, stretched out — '

Grace shook her head.

'What needs to be done, Carey, we'll do together. I shan't faint at the sight of blood.'

They dismounted and hitched the horses and Carey walked towards the house. The girl braced herself, then followed. Roger Hammond lay on the veranda, his face strangely calm in death; his eyes had lost their brightness, and his hands were stained with red where he had held them to his chest.

Grace wanted to cry; she fought back the tears. A fierce desire for revenge flamed through her; she conquered it — justice, not revenge was what the valley needed. She must wait for the sheriff to arrive and let the law take its course.

'We'll take him into the house,' she said quietly.

Carey, nodding, placed his hands under Hammond's armpits.

'You take his ankles, Grace.'

They carried him inside and placed him on a sofa. Grace got some water and washed the blood from her father's hands. Carey placed a white sheet over him.

There was a long silence. The house

felt as if no one had ever lived there, or ever would. Grace clenched her hands until her nails dug into the flesh of her palms.

Carey said: 'There's still Cookie.'

They went outside and across the yard. The cook, a fat man with cheeks that had been rosy-red and were now pale, lay on the ground, a revolver still tightly clutched in his right hand. Carey had some difficulty in removing the gun. They carried him into the barn — it was nearer than the house — and laid him out on a board on trestles. Grace washed the dirt from his face and covered him over.

'We'll bring the minister out tomorrow,' Grace said, 'and bury them under the pines. You'd better get back to the cattle now — Dyson may come again.'

Carey hesitated.

'I didn't ought to leave yuh here alone, Miss Hammond.'

'I'll be all right. If Dyson attacks again, it'll be at the herd, not here. And someone has to cook for the men — I'll be too busy to fret.'

Carey was still reluctant to leave, but he saw it was no good arguing with her. He mounted his horse.

'Just one thing,' he said. 'I want to be in the party that goes after Dyson — you'll let me know when the posse forms?'

'I'll let you know,' the girl replied. 'And I'll be driving out with some food for the men as soon as I get it ready.'

Carey wheeled his horse about and rode away. Grace watched him out of sight, then turned back to the house. She stood over her father, a great sadness inside her. Now that she was alone, she cried; the tears streamed down her face.

'Oh, Pete — Pete,' she whispered. 'Come back to me. Don't leave me alone now. I need you.'

She remembered that she had hungry men to feed and went to the kitchen. The cook had been preparing meat and potatoes when Dyson had struck; his knife lay on the table near a side of

197

beef. Mechanically, Grace Hammond continued his work.

She cut the meat and potatoes into slices and placed the pieces in a metal tray; she stoked up the fire under the oven. She worked slowly, with a heavy heart, without interest. The house was quiet and time passed without meaning.

She put the food on to cook and sat down. Outside, it was growing dark, the first flakes of snow beginning to fall. Low clouds hinted that there might be a heavy fall.

Somewhere, far off, the harsh rattle of gunfire started up. Grace Hammond came to her feet, alert. She listened a moment, and went outside to study the wind. Yes, there could be no doubt — the shots came from the direction of the basin. Dyson must be raiding the herd.

Calmly, she went back inside the house and lifted down a rifle from the wall. She opened a drawer and pulled out a handful of cartridges. She loaded the gun and walked to the front door. This was her fight. It was her range and her men shooting it out with the rustlers. She could not leave them leaderless . . . not against the men who had murdered her father.

As she reached the porch, two men rode into the patio. She did not recognise them immediately for the sky was dark with snow-clouds. But one of them recognised her, and called:

'Grace!'

She knew that voice; Fingle's voice. What was he doing here? Carey had said he was one of those who had shot down her father — her gun came up, covering Fingle. She saw the other man then; a slim man in a crimson jacket, with curly black hair and snake-like eyes. Claude Dyson!

Grace snapped: 'I've got you covered. Don't try anything or I'll fire. Get off your horses and walk towards me, slowly, with your arms above your heads.'

Fingle said, in alarm: 'Don't shoot, Grace — '

Dyson ignored her. Perhaps he couldn't take the idea of a gun in the hands of a woman seriously. He stared at a brown mare hitched to the rail, and said:

'That is Stoat's horse. What's going on here?'

Grace told him.

'I borrowed it after Pete Marsh killed him.'

Fingle went white.

'Marsh is still alive? Here?'

Dyson's eyes fixed on the slender figure of the girl. He looked past her, to left and right. His body was tense; if Marsh were here . . .

'You didn't think Pete would run from one of you?' Grace said scornfully. 'He's gone for the sheriff and — '

Dyson smiled.

'So you're alone, Miss Hammond — how nice!'

Grace saw she'd made a mistake, too late. Dyson's hands blurred with the speed of his gundraw. Grace fired, but Dyson was quicker. His slug struck the barrel of her rifle, driving it sideways in her hands. She missed, and staggered back. Dyson was off his horse and coming for her. Grace stepped back into the house and slammed the door. She ran for the window, smashed the glass with her rifle and fired into the patio. Dyson ducked for cover; Fingle was nowhere to be seen.

There was silence, no movement from the gathering darkness. Grace pushed fresh shells into the magazine, and waited. Another burst of gunfire sounded away at the basin; Dyson must have left his men to raid the herd while he returned to the house. She wondered why he had come back.

Fingle's voice came: 'Grace, don't be silly. I shan't hurt you. You know how much I love you — come out here.'

She loosed off a shot in the direction of his voice.

'You'll hang for murdering my father, Fingle — if I don't kill you first!'

She heard them whispering together, then they split up, moving round the house. Grace had to keep tight hold on her nerves; she was alone with two killers and she could expect no help from her own riders — they were busy fighting for their lives. Fingle and Dyson evidently intended to creep up on her from behind.

She ran to the next room. This was a small place, with only one window and one door. She locked the door and barricaded it with a heavy desk, taking up a position to cover the window with her rifle. She could only wait, and hope.

Minutes passed. A dull crackle of sound from the back of the house worried her. The faint smell of burning wood drifted on the air. Grace felt the cold hand of fear grip her heart — they had set fire to the house and were going to burn her out.

The ranch-house was all-timber and burnt quickly. The flames roared noisily, throwing up a bright light. Dense smoke filtered into the room, almost choking the girl. She smashed the window to let in air. The door was ablaze. The ceiling began to sag. Clouds of hot smoke swirled about her, and the heat grew intense. Grace knew she had to get out of the house — and knew that Dyson and Fingle were waiting for her. She pushed her rifle through the window and fired randomly, then climbed through. Behind her, a blaze of light silhouetted her as she ran for the cover of the barns.

Fingle stepped from his hiding-place and grabbed her. He tore the rifle from her hands, holding her close, smiling down at her. His eyes gleamed in a way that made her shudder as he tried to kiss her. Grace struggled desperately to free herself.

Fingle cursed and held her tighter.

'Stop it, you little fool,' he said roughly. 'I'm not going to hurt you. I love you, Grace, and — '

She grabbed his Colt from its waist holster and tried to turn it on him, but he was stronger than she realised. He snatched the gun out of her hand and swung the barrel across her forehead.

Grace swayed, blackness engulfing her, and fell unconscious at his feet.

* * *

Pete Marsh turned on Carey, fierce anger raging inside him.

'You let Fingle get his hands on Grace?' he snarled. 'I ought to — '

Sheriff Brownsides pushed him back. 'Let's have the story,' he said curtly.

The crowd quietened on River Bend's Main Street. Horses were held in check. Snowflakes drifted through the flickering light of oil-lamps and darkness pressed down beyond the ring of men.

Carey said, tersely: 'I left Grace at the ranch and rode to the basin, to help with the cattle — those were Miss Hammond's orders. Dyson's men struck again, trying to run off the cattle, and there was a fight. I didn't see Dyson with them — Slim was in charge. Then I saw a fire in the distance; it was the ranch-house and I

204

remembered that Grace was still there.

'I left the fight and rode hell-for-leather. Dyson and Fingle were just leaving and the house was beyond saving. Fingle had Grace across his saddle; she had been knocked out or he'd never have held her, I reckon. I threw a gun on Dyson, but he's faster than me. He shot my horse and I took a fall. They made off with Miss Hammond, south, towards Dyson's territory. I was groggy for quite a while and, by the time I collected another horse, I'd lost them. So I got the boys together and came to town. We're leaving right away to settle that skunk for good!'

Doc Turner added. 'Dyson's had a free hand too long. I guess he made his big mistake in grabbing Miss Hammond — he's roused the whole town against him.'

Pete Marsh looked at Carey.

'Sorry,' he said. 'I spoke hastily. I'm not blaming you for what happened.'

An impatient voice broke through from the back of the crowd.

'What yuh waitin' for, sheriff? Let's get after them rats!'

Brownsides frowned.

'There ain't going to be no mob-rule about this,' he said loudly. 'I represent the law and Marsh is my deputy. I'm swearing in every man here as a legal member of my posse. You'll take my orders and like it. Dyson and the rest will have the chance to surrender and stand trial . . . and there will be no lynching party!'

Marsh said: 'We've got to get Grace away from them first.'

The sheriff nodded.

'Dyson having her in his power sure complicates the situation. We'll have to move carefully. I'm not taking the risk of anything happening to her.'

He stared grimly at the milling horsemen.

'All right men; sort yourselves out. Form a double file and raise yore right hands. Now, repeat after me . . . '

The Hammond riders and the men of River Bend took the oath.

'We're riding for the Dyson place,' Brownsides told them, 'and we're going quietly. I don't want anyone shooting off a gun till I give the word. We'll surround the place and try to get Miss Hammond out before the showdown. Let's go!'

Marsh and the sheriff headed the column of grim-faced men that rode out of River Bend. The posse moved at a fast canter, travelling through darkness and snow, south across the open prairie. The moon, showing through heavy cloud-banks, gave them a little light. The wind howled, driving into their faces.

'Sheriff,' Marsh said, raising his voice to be heard above the roar of the wind. 'Let me go on ahead. One man may be able to get to Miss Hammond.'

'Maybe,' Brownsides answered. 'We'll see how the land lies when we get there. You stick right beside me and remember you're a deputy under my orders.'

They rode on, passing bluffs and a belt of pine trees. The wind slowed the horses and the snow blinded them. It was nearing blizzard conditions. At first the weather had caused some of the men to curse; that had stopped. They had drawn up neckerchiefs over their nostrils and were fighting for breath. A bitter coldness seeped through Marsh's clothes, numbing him. He rode on doggedly, thinking only of Grace Hammond.

They reached the top of the rise overlooking Dyson's ranch, and stopped. Down below, through the swirl and flurry of snow, moonlight revealed the outline of a high wooden wall. Yellow light glowed behind the windows of the big house. The main gate was tight shut.

Sheriff Brownsides rubbed his eyes clear of snow and stared at the fortress. It was shaped as a triangle, with the base pointing north and the apex south.

He said: 'Turner, take ten men and move round to the left side. Carey, go to the right. Smith, you'll take charge of the rest and stay here. Marsh and I will try to sneak in and get to Miss Hammond. The signal to move in will be three shots close together. Everyone understand?'

'Sure, sheriff. Get moving before this blizzard freezes us solid!'

They waited till Turner and Carey had moved off to take up covering positions, then Marsh and the sheriff rode down the trail to the ranch. The path and the grassland were one white sheet, and the heavy snowfall would hide their approach to the ranch.

They were still twenty yards off when the gate slowly opened. Lights bobbed about in the yard. Shots came, singly, at random, but no one was aiming at Marsh or the sheriff. Some kind of trouble had broken out inside the ranch-house.

Marsh sweated, despite the cold, urging his horse forward. Grace was in danger, a voice screamed in his head. He must get to her.

Brownsides was beside him, trying to hold him back. A shadowy figure came running from the gateway, stumbled through the snow towards them. The sheriff grabbed for his gun.

Marsh shouted: 'Don't shoot — it's Miss Hammond!'

12

Finale

Grace came slowly back to consciousness, a dull throbbing in her temples
and a strange uneasiness troubling her.
She could not remember what had
happened. She sat up, holding her head
between her hands; her eyes began to
focus again, and she saw that she was in
a strange room, sitting on the edge of a
bed, facing a window. Beyond the
window, there was darkness and falling
snow.

An oil-lamp stood on the table and a
Mexican woman squatted on a mat on
the floor. She was a heavily built
woman with dark skin and greasy hair,
and she worked on a rope mat,
threading the strands with a bone awl.
Grace had never seen her before.

'Salud, senorita,' the Mexican said.

'You feel better, yes?'

Grace moved unsteadily from the bed, swaying a little. It seemed she must have woken in the middle of a nightmare.

'Where am I?' she asked uncertainly.

The Mexican smiled, showing broken yellow teeth.

'This is the ranch of Senor Dyson,' she answered, and the name brought back Grace Hammond's memory.

She remembered her father's death, Dyson firing the ranch, her struggle with Fingle. The ex-foreman had knocked her out with his gun barrel; he must have brought her here, a prisoner. Grace went cold with fear.

The Mexican woman rose from the mat leaving her work, and crossed to the door. She opened it, and called down the stairs:

'Senor Dyson. The girl has recovered.'

Grace tried to pull herself together. Now was not time for weakness; somehow, she must escape. Her head still ached and she knew that she must have an ugly bruise on her temples.

Voices sounded below, men's voices. She recognised Dyson's; there came crude laughter and feet on the stairs. Grace braced herself. It was not Dyson who came up, but Fingle. He came eagerly into the room, his eyes crawling over the girl's lovely figure. Grace shuddered, shrinking from him.

'Get out,' Fingle snapped at the Mexican. 'And leave us alone.'

The woman went out, and Fingle kicked the door shut. He stood looking at Grace, smiling, enjoying the moment. He had waited a long time to get her in his power.

'You needn't think anyone will save you, Grace,' he said. 'You've put me off long enough — now it's my turn. Dyson won't interfere. So far as he's concerned, you're just a hostage.'

Grace Hammond stood rigid, her face pale, her eyes cold as ice.

'Don't touch me, Fingle,' she said. 'Do you think I could ever care for you after you murdered my father?'

He laughed, moving towards her. His breath came quicker, and his hands reached out to grab her. Grace tried to duck past him, but he caught her arm and held her. He bent to kiss her. Grace brought up her free hand and slapped him across the face, hard, so that the blow left a white mark. She jerked herself free and backed to the wall, stood there quivering.

Fingle licked his lips.

'You've got spirit,' he admitted. 'I'm going to enjoy breaking you to my will!'

Grace said: 'You'd better get out now, Fingle. Pete Marsh will kill you for this.'

'I reckon Marsh is in gaol by this time,' the ex-foreman jeered. 'He's wanted by the law — remember? And if he ain't, Dyson has twenty gunmen downstairs — you think he can get anywhere near yuh?'

Grace was desperate. The light in Fingle's eyes showed unmistakably that he was near-crazy. He could think of nothing but her.

She said: 'The sheriff will be coming. Do you think he'll do nothing when he learns my father was murdered?'

She moved round the wall, trying to keep beyond the reach of Fingle's long arms. He followed her, playing cat to her mouse. There was stark fear in her, for the animal bestiality glowing in his face revealed a side of his character that he had kept hidden. Now she was seeing the real Fingle for the first time.

'The sheriff's got no proof,' he answered. 'We burnt down the ranch-house to destroy the bodies.'

Grace kept moving; Fingle followed her, but he never made the mistake of leaving the door unguarded. Always he was between her and the stairs. He lunged suddenly, springing forward and taking her by surprise. Grace went back and was trapped in a corner. Fingle held her, kissing her.

'Now, my beauty,' he said thickly, 'you've finished running! You're mine — mine!'

Fingle was not wearing his gunbelt but, on the floor, where the Mexican woman had been working on her mat, lay the bone awl. It was long and sharp, thick at one end and tapering to a point. Grace let her whole body go limp and, Fingle surprised, was not ready to take her weight. She broke his hold and fell to the floor, rolled over, half-crawling, reaching out for the weapon.

Her right hand closed round the awl as Fingle sprawled across her. And Grace, hardly aware of what she was doing, swung her hand and drove the needle-sharp awl into his body.

Fingle jerked once, convulsively, then slumped heavily. His face was ashen, and he moaned a little. The bone awl snapped, leaving Grace holding the thick end of it, the needle point deep in his heart. Grace pushed him off and struggled upright. She stood a moment, gasping for breath, leaning against the wall and expecting him to come after her again. But Fingle did not move.

He lay in a heap, his arms crumpled

under him, his eyes sightless. Only then did Grace Hammond realise that she had killed him. She felt sick and almost fainted.

Her brain reeled and she trembled violently. She had not meant to kill. Then she calmed. He was one of the men who had shot down her father in cold blood.

She opened the door and peered down the stairway. Men were drinking and playing cards in a room at the bottom. She heard Dyson's voice. Someone was singing in a drunken stupor. Grace closed the door quietly; she could not escape that way. She looked round the room, her eyes unconsciously avoiding the sight of Fingle's dead body.

There was the window. She crossed the room and opened it. Outside was darkness, a cold, singing wind and snow falling. Oil-lamps showed her that the yard was deserted, a high wall in the distance. She looked down at the ground below, glad that the room was only on the first floor. There was no other way; she had to drop from the ledge.

She climbed on to the ledge and lowered herself carefully against the wall, her feet scraping the timber. She hung a moment by her hands, then let go. She dropped, breathless, her legs doubling up as she hit the ground.

The wind-driven snow became a blinding blizzard, battering at her. She staggered upright and began to run for the gateway. Behind her, a shout came. Her escape had been discovered. A man appeared at the window; a gun showed and a shot came winging after her. Grace ran faster, keeping in shadow.

She was nearly at the gate when an uproar started from the house. Men came running out, some with lamps, some with guns. Lead spattered wildly about her and the shots echoed and re-echoed.

Fortunately, there was no guard on the gate; the weather had driven everyone to shelter. She fumbled with the latch as a bullet drove into the woodwork beside her. She got the gate open and ran out. Snowflakes danced in the wind and the prairie was black as night. Then two horsemen appeared before her and she heard Marsh's voice . . .

Pete Marsh slid from the saddle and caught her with his one good arm. He held her close as she swayed, sobbing:

'Pete — Pete — thank God you've come! I killed him — I killed Fingle! I didn't mean to. It was — '

Marsh steadied her.

'Don't worry about it, Grace — you only saved the hangman a job. Don't worry about a thing. You're safe now.'

Sheriff Brownsides was off his horse with a gun in his hand. The snow flurried about them, white and cold, driven on the wind. From inside the wall about Dyson's ranch, gunshots came. Brownsides returned the fire, triggering three times in quick succession — the signal for the posse to close in.

Hoofbeats sounded through the night. Riders were coming, shouting and firing off their guns. Marsh pulled the girl into the cover of the high wall.

'Stay there,' he told her. 'Stay there until I get back.'

He turned and ran to the gateway, to take his place beside the sheriff.

'We've got to keep the gate open,' Brownsides said — and fired again. A rustler fell, groaning.

Marsh had his Colt in his left hand, his right arm still bandaged and in a sling. He saved his lead for the showdown. Men were running about inside, not knowing what had happened. Then Dyson's voice sounded above the melee:

'It's the sheriff's posse. Get those lights out!'

One by one the flickering yellow flames went out. Pitch blackness descended — a blackness so intense that Marsh could only feel the snow, wet against his face, not see it. Crimson flashes streaked out. Gunshots boomed noisily. The smell of cordite fumes hung on the night air.

Suddenly, there was Smith and Joe Brett and half a dozen others riding into the gateway, loosing off lead. The foremost horse took a tumble and the others piled into it. Men came sliding out of the saddle, ducking for cover as Dyson's gunmen went into action.

The moon showed briefly, showed men running and shooting and falling. Gunfire started from a new direction — Turner and his men were climbing the east wall. Dyson shouted fresh orders:

'Back to the house — we can hold them from there!'

There was a scurry in the darkness, and more shooting. Someone moaned and writhed in agony; Carey dropped to the ground after climbing the west wall. He shouted to his men:

'After them, boys — this is the showdown!'

Marsh had lost contact with the sheriff. He pushed forward, searching for Claude Dyson. Dyson was the cause of the trouble and Marsh wanted to deal with him personally. He pressed through the milling cowboys, gun in hand and a grim light in his eyes.

The moon came again and, without warning, he found himself face to face with Slim. Recognition was mutual. Slim snarled: 'Marsh!' and threw up his gun for a killing shot. Marsh fired from his hip, wounded Slim and ran on, swinging his gun barrel to knock the outlaw off his feet. Somewhere, he heard Brownsides shouting:

'Get under cover. Surround the house and hold your fire!'

The moon went behind the clouds and there was darkness again. The wind was still rising, driving icy sheets of snow and sleet across the yard. Dyson's men were comfortably set in the house; the posse were going to have a bad time unless they could finish the job quickly.

Marsh tucked his Colt under his injured arm and reloaded. He wondered how Grace was. Sheriff Brownsides stepped from cover, cupping his hands over his mouth to shout:

'Dyson. This is the law. I call on you and yore men to surrender. Throw down your guns and come out with yore hands high. You'll get a fair trial.'

A volley of lead streaked from the house, forcing the sheriff to duck for shelter. Someone laughed, and a voice said:

'Go to hell, the lot of yuh!'

Marsh, crouching low, shivered. The cold and wet was beginning to seep into his bones. It seemed impossible to break into the house, yet they could not maintain a siege all night; by morning they would be frozen to death. He remembered what Grace had said when Fingle had named him outlaw . . . 'We have to fight fire with fire.' And Dyson had burnt down the Hammond ranch. Fire was the answer now. Fire to burn out the rats, fire to give warmth, and light to see by.

Marsh stumbled through the darkness. He ran into someone — the moon showed again and he saw it was Lefty.

'This way, Lefty — to the stables. Help me carry hay to the back of the house. We'll fire it and burn them out!'

The cowboy grunted agreement and followed after Marsh. They found the stables and flung wide the doors; inside Dyson's horses were moving restively, upset by the shooting. Along one wall, a long trough was filled with dry grass.

Marsh said: 'We shan't be able to control the fire in this wind, so turn the horses loose. 'Sides, we don't want to give those crooks inside the house a chance to ride off.'

Lefty released the horses and drove them into the yard. A fresh exchange of gunfire between Dyson's outfit and the posse startled the horses; they panicked and bolted through the open gateway, galloping wildly over the prairie.

'Now,' said Marsh in a satisfied tone, 'to deal with Claude Dyson!'

He and Lefty carried armfuls of hay to the rear of the house. Under the cover of darkness, they made several trips, piling the hay high against the timber walls of the building.

'Should be enough to start a fine blaze,' Lefty grunted.

Marsh struck a match on the sole of his boots. The wind blew it out. He cursed shortly and struck another. The hay smouldered. The wind caught the sparks and spread them.

Brownsides' voice sounded again, shouting to the house:

'You coming out, Dyson? Or do we come in and get yuh?'

Gunshots boomed through the night. Jagged streaks of red flame stabbed the darkness. A cowboy dropped in the snow and lay still.

Lefty said: 'They'll be coming out, any time now!'

The hay burnt furiously, the flames caught at the wooden frame of the house and licked hungrily upwards. The wind fanned the fire to a blaze. In seconds, the house was alight, the heat driving Marsh and Lefty back.

The crackle of the flames turned to a

wild roar. Smoke poured out in great clouds, and a circle of bright light spread quickly across the yard.

Marsh shouted: 'Get back to the wall. Take cover and wait for them.'

There came a lull in the shooting as the posse retreated to take up new positions. The whole of the ranch-house was one sheet of flame; in minutes it would cease to exist. Then Dyson's gunmen came out running . . .

Some came out shooting, to die as the posse caught them in a crossfire. Others ran out with their arms above their heads, calling for mercy. Others, wounded, crawled from the inferno.

Marsh kept moving, hunting for the ring-leader. Where was Dyson? Had he been trapped in the house, or —

Brownsides shouted: 'Get back, boys! The fire's spreading — the wall is alight. Outside, everybody!'

The gale had driven sparks from the burning house to the barns and corrals; from there it spread like a wild thing to the high wooden wall surrounding

Dyson's fortress. In blinding snow, punchers and townsmen and rustlers ran for safety — to be trapped inside the blazing wall spelt death for all. Marsh, caught up in the surge through the gateway, looked for Grace and Dyson. He wanted to help the girl to safety; and he wanted Dyson . . .

He saw the leader of the outlaws running for a horse. In the confusion, Dyson had broken the ring formed by Brownsides' posse and was intent on escape.

Pete Marsh, thin-lipped and cursing, pushed his way through the melee and ran after Dyson. He brought up his Colt with his left hand, calling:

'I want you, Dyson! You're my prisoner. Throw up yore hands and surrender.'

Dyson, almost at the horse, turned, grabbing for his guns. He made a slight, effeminate figure outlined by the fire. His eyes glinted hatred. Stripped of his dandyish façade, he looked what he was — a killer, cold and cruel, ready to strike down the man who had ruined him. He saw the star on Marsh's chest, and laughed. Here was one lawman who would never take him!

His pearl-handled guns spat flame and lead. Marsh staggered, hit in the side, but he did not lose his balance or his purpose. His left arm came up level, the muzzle of his gun centred on Dyson's chest, aiming for the gleam of white shirt between the open crimson jacket. He squeezed the trigger once.

Dyson shuddered, took a half-step back and dropped. He did not move again.

Pete Marsh felt a weakness in his side. His eyes clouded, his head swam. Dyson's bullet must have hit him harder than he'd thought. He stumbled, even as friendly arms reached out to support him, and fell unconscious to the ground.

After Dyson's death, the fight did not last long. Their stronghold burnt out and their horses lost, the rustlers surrendered to take their chance with the law's trial. It was a strange procession that moved back to River Bend. The posse mounted, the outlaws walking, roped together, the injured on crude sleds fashioned from aspen branches. They moved slowly through the blizzard, back to town . . . but Marsh knew nothing of that.

He woke in Doc Turner's house, in bed, with Grace Hammond looking down at him, smiling. Sheriff Brownsides was there too. Marsh struggled to a sitting position and grinned wryly.

'Looks like I spend most of my time having slugs dug out of me,' he said, 'but it has its compensation — like having you for a nurse, Grace!'

She hugged him, her eyes moist with happiness.

'Everything's worked out for us, Pete,' she told him. 'Dyson's outfit is finished and there'll be peace through the valley again. I'm keeping the cattle and most of the land. And you're a free man again . . . '

Marsh looked at the sheriff for confirmation. Brownsides nodded.

'That's right, Marsh. I've sent in a report about you, and I don't doubt that all charges will be dropped. You did a good job as my deputy and I've a feeling Miss Hammond will see you keep right side of the law now.'

'I will,' Grace said determinedly. 'Starting right away! I'm marrying him before anything else happens to come between us.'

Turner cleared his throat.

'Looks like we're not wanted here, sheriff. Grace, don't — '

A knock at the door interrupted him.

Grace said, in a business-like way:

'I'd be obliged if you and the sheriff will stay a while longer, Doc. That'll be the minister at the door. We'll need you as witnesses!'

The way she hurried to the door told Pete Marsh his roving days were over; well, he'd come back to Gunsmoke Valley to marry and settle down — and it looked as if that was what was going to happen to him whether he liked it or not. He lay back and sighed contentedly. The new year was not far off, and a new life, with Grace beside him.

THE END

We do hope that you have enjoyed
reading this large print book.

Did you know that all of our titles
are available for purchase?

We publish a wide range of high
quality large print books including:
Romances, Mysteries, Classics
General Fiction
Non Fiction and Westerns

Special interest titles available in
large print are:
The Little Oxford Dictionary
Music Book, Song Book
Hymn Book, Service Book

Also available from us courtesy of
Oxford University Press:
Young Readers' Dictionary
(large print edition)
Young Readers' Thesaurus
(large print edition)

For further information or a free
brochure, please contact us at:
Ulverscroft Large Print Books Ltd.,
The Green, Bradgate Road, Anstey,
Leicester, LE7 7FU, England.
Tel: (00 44) 0116 236 4325
Fax: (00 44) 0116 234 0205

Other titles in the
Linford Western Library:

GUNS OF VIRTUE

Peter Wilson

Following the murder of his father, and his brother's decline into lawlessness, Adam Wade seeks revenge on the man he holds responsible. His search takes him to the town of Virtue, where ranch owner Hal Kember is a future state governor. But Adam becomes embroiled in a web of deceit and murder involving Kember's wife, Laura, his son, Luke, and a group of stage robbers and killers. In a final shoot-out there is one last life-changing shock for Adam.

LOPEZ'S LOOT

David Bingley

They were cousins, riding partners: Drifter, a white American, and Lopez — half-Mexican, travelling the southern border trails of the USA. Their money-raising schemes were often shady, sharing the risks and rewards: like the time Drifter turned in his 'wanted' partner, Lopez, and later sprung him. However, things changed when loot, in the form of church treasures, came their way. Clashing with posses and renegades their lives were at risk. Could they ever gain a more settled way of life?